Boonesborough Attack

Charles E. Hayes

Charles E. Hayes

DEDICATION

Friends Groups of Fort Boonesborough State Park, Blue Licks Battlefield State Resort Park and Fort Harrod State Park. To the young re-enactors Jimmy Schneider and Tommy Schneider because these young people appreciate history.

Picture by Jim Cummings, graphicenterprises.net

Picture by Jim Cummings, graphicenterprises.net

CONTENTS

Other Books by this author:

Kentucky Memories

Out of the Jungle

Gideon Strikes

Ambush at Blue Licks

Listening to night Winds at Blue Licks

The Bloody Sevens

Gideon Strikes (December 2014)

ACKNOWLEDGMENTS

The artist **Andrew Knez** for the use of his painting, *First Boonesborough Attack,* for the cover art. **Anne Crabb** for her magnificent information book, *The Battle Began Like a Clap of Thunder,* and **The Filson Club** for just being there.

Prologue

FORT BOONESBOROUGH was began on April 1 1775 by Daniel Boone and the men who had helped him blaze the trace between Martin's Station and Cumberland Gap and then from Cumberland Gap to the Kentucky River where we built Boonesborough.

My name is Samuel Walter and I was there with Boone at the beginning. I have been in Kentucky the past forty years and intend to stay in Kentucky.

We had all been hired by Judge Richard Henderson and the Transylvania Company to first blaze the trace and then to build a fort. Henderson and the Transylvania Company had bought Kentucky from the Cherokee at Sycamore Shoals earlier that spring. Henderson aimed to settle Kentucky as a proprietary colony with himself and the Transylvania Company receiving annual rents from the settlers.

Any of the Cherokee signers of the treaty of Sycamore Shoals could have told anyone who would have cared to ask, that they did not own the territory they sold and could not have held it if they had owned it. I figure that Henderson knew this but needed something he could argue in court if it ever came to that. The Cherokee maybe figured that if the settlers went to Kentucky to the north that they might be left alone in the area south of Kentucky.

Not all of the Cherokee felt this way. A young leader named Dragging Canoe not only refused to sign the treaty that sold Kentucky, he threatened settlers who would go to Kentucky saying they would find Kentucky a "dark and bloody land."

Before the treaty, Dragging Canoe got the Cherokee all riled up with a fiery and passionate speech. He was against any and all dealings with the white men and said: *"Whole Indian Nations have melted away like snowballs in the sun before the white man's advance. They leave scarcely a name of our people except those wrongly recorded by their destroyers. Where are the Delewares? They have been reduced to a mere shadow of their former greatness. We had hoped that the white men would not be willing to travel beyond the mountains. Now that hope is gone. They have passed the mountains, and have settled upon Tsalagi (Cherokee) land. They wish to have that usurpation sanctioned by treaty. When that is gained, the same encroaching spirit will lead them upon other land of the Tsalagi (Cherokees). New cessions will be asked. Finally the whole country, which the Tsalagi (Cherokees) and their fathers have so long occupied, will be demanded, and the remnant of the Ani Yvwiya, The Real People, once so great and formidable, will be compelled to seek refuge in some distant wilderness. There they will be permitted to stay only a short while, until they again behold the advancing banners of the same greedy host. Not being able to point out any further retreat for the miserable Tsalagi (Cherokees), the extinction of the whole race will be proclaimed. Should we not therefore run all risks, and incur all consequences, rather than to submit to further loss of our country? Such treaties may be alright for men who are too old to hunt or fight. As for me, I have my young warriors about me. We will hold our land. A-WANINSKI, I have spoken."*[1]

Even though he wasn't an established leader and was in his early twenties, Dragging Canoe's speech got some of the Cherokee all fired up and caused older leaders to close the treaty council. Henderson wasn't to be outdone by a speech no matter how powerful it was given. He acted quickly and responded by presenting the Cherokee leaders with a feast that included a lot of

[1] http://www.aaanativearts.com/cherokee/dragging-canoe.htm Alexander Cameron wrote down Dragging Canoe's speech, which became known as the "We are not yet conquered" speech.

rum. During the feasting and rum drinking, Henderson was able to persuade the chiefs to return to the treaty talks to talk over selling Kentucky to Henderson and the Transylvania Land Company.

Henderson knew that the Cherokee leaders favored the trade. He had sent Daniel Boone in ahead to dicker with them and make sure they were all in agreement with his terms. I always figured that the main reason Dragging Canoe was against the treaty and trade was to set himself up as a different leader and get himself a following. Whether that was his idea or not, that is what happened.

I reckon that Attakullakulla, Dragging Canoe's father, (he was also known as Little Carpenter, Leaning Wood and White Owl) was the highest ranking Chief of the Cherokee in 1775 and had been since about 1760. What's more, he supported selling of Kentucky to Henderson. More than he supported the sale, Attakullakulla supported peace. Attakullakulla had experienced both war and peace. He preferred peace over war as did another of his sons, Raven.

Henderson and the Transylvania Company wound up buying around twenty million acres of land from the Cherokee for two thousand pounds sterling and goods that were easy worth another eight thousand pounds. Dragging Canoe did not sign the treaty and promised Richard Henderson that Kentucky was going to be a "dark and bloody land."

Most of this I heard about later because even before the treaty was signed, I was with Daniel Boone and the rest of his party on our way to Kentucky to begin blazing the Boone Trace. We began blazing the trace at Martin's Station. Our work was real steady but wasn't near as demanding as some of the work I'd had to do in the past. We just followed a trail that Boone was already familiar with and removed the small saplings and bushes that could hinder travel. We blazed trees by cutting away bark to make the trace easier to stay on and follow. Boone was careful to place the trace by good camping places near water. Boone and all of us in his trace blazing party were receiving land for our efforts and we knew that our benefactor and employer would be following the trace behind us. Travel and work did not challenge any man in the party at first. We passed through Cumberland Gap. We crossed the Cumberland River and blazed a trace that took us to a pleasant spot named Raccoon Springs. From Raccoon Springs we blazed the trace to the Hazel Patch. After leaving the Hazel Patch, we forded the Rockcastle River.

That is where the harder work commenced. After crossing the Rockcastle, we sweated and blistered through about twenty miles or more of hard going through country that was thickly covered with dry dead brush. The work of our party was suddenly no longer minor cutting, clearing and blazing. It became a hard and brutal work. At the end of the dead brush, we had around thirty miles of thick cane and reeds to deal with. This was easier work but the cane grew thick and high. When we arrived at the edge of the cane, we could see the beautiful Kentucky plains. The land we viewed was beautiful and was highly rewarding to look upon. The richness and beauty brought a thrill and excitement to me and every man in the party.

We were bone tired. We were happy to be where we were. We were leaving the rugged mountains of Kentucky behind us and we had seen no Indian sign. We camped on a clear waterway without posting sentinels.

We turned in to get our sleep. I remember that Bull, my dog, stretched out close to me and I hoped he wouldn't get too close and disturb my sleep.

Bull did wake me. About an hour before daylight, I was awakened by a low deep growl from Bull. I reached for my rifle, powderhorn and pouch. Another dog, Twitty's I think, began barking. I moved so that my back was covered by a tree and was letting my eyes get used to the darkness when an uneven volley of what sounded like trade guns fire. Everyone who was able moved away from the source of the gunfire. I was already in position and the formed around me.

Boone began softly whispering every man's name. Each man except Twitty and his slave responded that he was ok except for Felix Walker who responded, "I'm wounded."

While it was still dark we heard a commotion at Twitty's tent. His dog was raising all kinds of hell then there was only the sound of some of our horses being ridden away.

We later discovered that Twitty's dog was able to protect him until a Shawnee tomahawk killed the dog. I do not think Twitty would have survived the first attack if his dog hadn't tried to protect him.

The attack noises ended as soon as the Indians were able to steal several horses. We came out of hiding and posted a defense around the camp, which I guess we should have done the night before. We buried Sam. We threw up lean-tos to shelter our wounded and for protection. Boone sent back a message to Henderson urging him to come with more men in a great haste. Twitty soon died from his wounds and Walker was carried to the Kentucky River, where the fort at Boonesborough was built.

Fort Boonesborough began as a small stockade that was expanded in 1776 to a 250 feet by 150 feet walled community. The kidnapping of Jemima Boone and the Callaway girls along with other Indian threats encouraged the settlers to erect a strong palisade with blockhouses at each of the four corners.

During 1776, the settler population of Kentucky grew to over a thousand settlers but by the spring of 1777, there were no more than three hundred settlers in Kentucky

Indian raids caused several stations to close and the people to flee to east of the mountains. In January 1777. McConnell's Station was forced to close and other's followed. Fort Harrod was attacked and it was later discovered that almost five hundred Shawnee were camped about a quarter mile from the fort. The fort was attacked during the spring of 1777, the year of the terrible sevens or the bloody sevens. Two settlers were killed and several, including Boone, were wounded. Boone was only saved because a settler from the Limestone area by the name of Simon Butler picked him up and carried him into the fort,[2] When notes were found pinned to slain settlers telling them that they would be rewarded for joining the British, the settlers realized that the British were helping finance the Indian raids into Kentucky. The ever constant presence of Shawnee during 1777 kept settlers close to the fort.

Logan's Fort was attacked in May and June. The Shawnee seemed to be focusing on one fort at a time but no fort was ever lacking in attention from the Shawnee.

The arrival of Colonel Bowman and a hundred militiamen from Virginia lessened the pressure from the Shawnee but didn't end it entirely.

The arrival of winter was welcomed by the settlers. It was hoped that the colder weather would keep the Shawnee closer to their village fires and out of Kentucky. Winter also brought the realization that very little had been raised in the way of crops due to the constant harassment by the Shawnee. To make matters worse, few supplies had been brought from the east.

In late 1776, I had returned to North Carolina and had brought back a wife, Patsy.

---

[2] Simon Butler was the name used by Simon Kenton when he thought he was wanted for murdering a man in a fist fight.

Patsy O'Reilly had been an indentured servant from Ireland. In return for staking out a claim for her owner, building a lean-to and planting a crop of corn on it; I bought Patsy's release. Some would say that by buying her indenture, that I owned her. I never felt that way for a minute and I don't reckon she did either.

Patsy was generally easy to talk to and get along with. She did have a spell of temper just as I was getting ready to go hunting after Boone and others went to the Blue Licks to boil down salt.

Picture by Jim Cummings, graphicenterprises.net

1

PATSY

February 1778

Patsy sat on a split log bench and stared at the fire. She clutched a Lindsey-Woolsey shirt to the right side of her face. She was all cried out. She had cried so much that it would not have surprised her if she was never able to cry again. Now she felt numb. She was so numb that she could not tell that her back was cold and that the front of her that faced the fire was too hot.

The shirt and Samuel's rifle, pouch and powderhorn had been brought to her hours earlier. Two men from the fort had found the items hidden in a hollow tree with the help of Bull, Samuel's dog. Patsy knew that while the men took the credit for finding the items, that Bull deserved all the credit.

Samuel had left to take supplies to the salt makers and was supposed to hunt on his way back to the fort. He left alone. Bull was forced to stay behind because he had hurt his right front paw and Samuel didn't want to risk laming the dog. Bull was better and Patsy thought that it would have been better to wait for Bull to heal instead of being in such an all fired hurry to leave.

Patsy figured that all men were stupid. Let a man's wife be just a little out of sorts and they had to either get flustered or go hunting. Patsy felt that Samuel should have known without being told that she was pregnant. Margaret had known almost as soon as Patsy had known,

Margaret Taylor, a twenty-five year old mother of three living children, sat beside her and hugged her. Patsy pushed her face into the shirt and sobbed again.

Margaret had intended to tell Patsy she needed her help preparing supper. At the very least, she needed to be able to use the fire that Patsy was sitting in front of to cook a meal.

"Margaret, are all men blind and stupid?"

"Oh yes. All of them."

"Even Ben?"

"I think sometimes that Ben aint got a lick of sense."

"Margaret, they didn't find him. Maybe he's still alive."

"Aint likely. His gun was still loaded and there was a lot of Indian sign.

"But they didn't find him."

"There was fresh snow over everything," Margaret explained patiently,

"But .... "

"And it was still snowing ..."

"But ..."

"Patsy, you don't need to help with supper tonight. You

just climb up to your bed in the loft and rest yourself for a while."

While she spoke, Margaret helped Patsy up and guided her to the ladder leading to the loft. Margaret knew that Patsy was beyond being any help and wanted to give her a chance to grieve without being on display for anyone who came into the cabin.

Working quickly and with practiced skill, Margaret had a pan of cornbread covered with embers to cook and a kettle stew warming in the fireplace. She called her oldest son to the cabin and gave him a bucket to fetch fresh water in and sat down when he returned with the water.

"Ma, Jemima Callaway said that she could feed us if you wanted to get shut of us at supper time."

"Tell her I said thanky."

Margaret was very thankful. Patsy was young, barely seventeen and was, at this time, very needful. Seventeen year old wives were not unusual on the Kentucky Frontier. In fact, Margaret didn't know of any seventeen year old female in Kentucky who wasn't either a wife or a widow. She had heard that Jacob Hensley's daughter had arrived at Logan's Fort unmarried but that didn't last long. Single women on the frontier were scarce to the point of being nonexistent. Bachelors, on the other hand, outnumbered single women by at least ten to one, and that was before Colonel Bowman arrived in Kentucky with a hundred single militiamen.

Margaret had no sooner reflected on these facts that there was a knock and the sound of scuffling at the cabin door. Opening the door, Margaret stepped aside to avoid being pushed down by three men who each were trying to be the first to enter the cabin.

"Ezekiel, David, and James what has got into you three?"

David was the first to answer. "Margaret, I was coming over here to offer condolences to Miss Patsy and court her. These men tried to push me out of the way."

"Look at him!" Ezekiel exclaimed. "He aint even shaved and him thinking to call on Miss Patsy."

Ezekiel had shaved and in a hurry. His face showed where he had nicked himself several times.

"Miss Margaret, I took time me to shave and to wash up," interjected James. "As cold as it is, I washed up. I reckon that should allow me to court her first."

Margaret answered the three men with a voice heavy with scorn. "Ezekiel, you were first. David, you shaved and you James, both shaved and washed up. And you each think you should be allowed to court a woman who only found out today that her husband is dead. What makes you think that any of you three got enough sense to court a woman?"

Neither of the three replied which was just as well because Margaret was just getting warmed up. Her face flushed a bright red as she continued, "You hear about a new widow and the first thing you think about is to come sniffing around like a bunch of dogs after a bitch in heat. You don't give her time to finish her crying and grieving before you come over here to pester after her and to get in my way?"

Grabbing a broom, Margaret demanded, "Can you tell me one reason that I shouldn't beat you all like the dogs you're acting like?"

John drew himself up to his full height and tried to answer. "Now Miss Patsy will have to choose somebody. She can't just stay not married. What can she do, bound herself to somebody as a servant? If it aint us here courting her, it will be somebody else."

13

"Miss Patsy, Miss Patsy, Miss Patsy, Miss Patsy, Miss Patsy. Don't you mean Mrs. Walter? I'll let it be known when men can come here a courting. Now you three scat out of here before I bring hurt down on you all. Besides, my oldest boy is almost eleven years old. Maybe it is time for him to study about taking him a wife."

With that, Margaret swung her broom and the three men rapidly retreated from the cabin. Margaret checked the food and adjusted the fire. The smell of the stew and the cornbread began to fill the cabin. Margaret started to climb the ladder to the loft to comfort but decided Patsy would be better off left alone for a while.

In the loft, Patsy lay on her bed feeling more numb than she had ever felt before. She had heard everything that had been said in the cabin. She couldn't have missed it since the inside of the cabin was only twelve by seventeen feet and the loft was twelve by twelve feet. The loft was where she and Samuel had slept with the three Taylor boys. The two sleeping areas were separated by stacks of supplies and anything that needed to be stored. Even with the supplies separating the two sleeping areas, Patsy always felt uneasy when she and Samuel coupled. She felt like not just the Taylors but the whole fort could hear them. She heard Margaret and Ben almost every night.

She heard Ben enter the cabin. She knew without looking that he would be carrying an armload of firewood. Ben never entered the cabin without bringing firewood or a bucket of water with him. Lying on her bed, Patsy heard Ben put the firewood by the fireplace and walk over to Margaret.

"Looked to me like Ezekiel, David and John were pretty eager to get out of here."

"Ben, do you know what those sons of bitches were doing?"

"I allowed they were coming a courtin."

"And you think that was okay."

Ben pulled her to him and lifted her chemise so that his hands were on the bare skin of her hips. He leaned down and kissed her on the neck beneath her left ear and whispered, "Oh yes, and I am dead set in favor of courtin. In fact, I'm in favor of a little courtin right now."

Ben backed Margaret to their bed and eased her back on to the straw filled tick that covered the hickory slats. He continued giving her soft kisses and whispered, "I favor courtin a whole lot."

Despite her irritation, Margaret wiggled her clothing above her hips and helped him pull his suspenders and breeches down. Soon, Patsy could hear their heavy breathing and the rhythmic creaking of their bed while they made love.

Patsy O'Reilly had arrived in North Carolina from Ireland with her parents and brother when she was twelve years old. Her parents and brother had been indentured to a family with a big farm who didn't like having African slaves. Patsy had been indentured to another farmer and his wife who lived twenty-five miles away, primarily to care for the farmer's mother as well as helping with cooking and housework. The work wasn't particularly hard but is was demanding as the indenture holder's mother was in a great deal of pain and was therefore very impatient.

Patsy met Samuel when she was fourteen and he was nineteen. Jack O'Hara, the owner of her papers would invest in Samuel's long hunts and apparently made a profit every time that he did. Samuel and Patsy talked when they had a chance. He reminded her of her father and uncles. He was serious but had a ready smile and listened when she spoke. When Samuel asked if he could marry her, the farmer said that he would have to buy out the remainder of her indenture before they could be married. It was then that the arrangement for Samuel to go with Boone to Kentucky and establish a claim for O'Hara in exchange for the rest of Patsy's indenture.

Patsy was pleased with the arrangement at first but gradually began to think of herself as property again. She had arrived in America and separated from her family at the age of twelve. She married Samuel when she was sixteen and went with him to Boonesborough. Patsy had begun to feel that she was missing out on something – maybe a lot of something's. Now, at the age of seventeen, she was a widow and about to be a mother. This feeling that she was missing out on something added to the non-private nature of their physical relations and the fact that Samuel did not know that she was expecting a child caused her to begin to find fault with Samuel. Now Samuel was dead. The man who would hold her close at night and touch her gently was dead. She tried to smell Samuel in the shirt she held to her face.

Now men were coming to court her. She was expected to marry one of them. Her only other option was to indenture herself or be a servant. She rightly suspected that no wife would want a seventeen year old woman in her house whether as a paid servant or as an indentured servant. She had noticed that married women seemed almost as anxious to get single women over the age of fourteen married as the men were anxious to marry them.

Patsy felt helpless as she wondered if she was going to be owned by another man whether she wanted it or not. She didn't like feeling helpless. She wished desperately that she had realized before how much she loved Samuel.

2

ESCAPED

SEPTEMBER 1778

"Don't shoot, damn it, he's a white man."

"Get this damn dog off of me."

I was jarred awake to the sound of a dog growling and two men yelling. When I say awake, I am exaggerating. I had traveled most of the night and sat down to rest when it was just beginning to get first light. Looking through half opened eyes, I judged my sleep to have been no more than two and a half to three hours. To be honest, I wasn't sure if I was awake or dreaming. I shook my head to try to clear the fog away and opened my eyes. I saw one man trying to level a rifle at me and a dog that looked too familiar not to be in a dream doing his best to stop him. Another man was trying to separate the dog from the first man. I tried to stand but I was only able to raise myself up to my hands and knees. I tried twice and had to shake my head again to clear it before I was able to speak. I called to the dog.

"Bull!"

Bull ran to me and began licking my face. That was enough to convince me that this was not a dream and that I needed to wake up fast. I tried to get to get up again and had to use my walking stick to help me stand upright. Two strangers were facing me but their rifles were no longer pointed at me so I wasn't too worried. Both wore patched buckskin breeches but the man who Bull had a disagreement with was now wearing ripped breeches. I noticed that the men were both paying real close attention to the forest around them.

"Stranger, who might you be?" questioned the man with the ripped breeches, "and how did you come to know Bull?"

I was still struggling to keep on standing up. I had to lean hard on my walking stick before I could stand fully upright. The two men start forward to help me until they were stopped real short by a protective, growling, and ferociously snarling Bull. Bull wasn't the biggest dog and usually wasn't the meanest dog. Bull was, however, one of the most loyal dogs on the Kentucky frontier. His lineage and breed was anybody's guess. What was dead sure certain was that he was protecting me, just as he had before.

"Stranger, I'm George Tyrie and this is my brother Simon. Now tell us who you are and why Bull has sudden turned against us. We've been hunting with Bull for a month now."

"I am Samuel Walter and Bull is my dog."

"Well I'll be damned. Look, if we'd knowed you was a white man, we wouldn't never have studied about killing you. It's just that you damn sure look like an Injun."

I looked down at my body. I was bare except for the cover of a breechclout and moccasins. Not only was I almost naked, I was dark from constant exposure to the sun and weather.

George continued, "Why, if it wasn't for you needing a shave, I wouldn't have had any idea that you was a white man."

I agreed with him. I nodded, "I forgot what I must look like.

I escaped from the Shawnee four days ago and have barely stopped moving since I left them. I reckon I have got tireder than I thought"

"You come all this way afoot?"

"No. I had a horse that got lamed too bad to use sometime after we crossed the Ohio River."

"I heard about you. They found your rifle and shirt in a follow tree."

"I hid them there. I figured that if the Shawnee found me, there weren't no use giving them a good shirt and my gear. I figured that somebody might come looking for me and I figured they would bring Bull to try to find me. I knew Bull would find the shirt I had been wearing. When the men got the shirt, they would get my rifle and my gear too. Main thing was to keep the Shawnee from getting them."

"How did you manage to stay alive?"

"When I saw I was going to get caught, I hollered at them and walked right to them. I showed them an old map of Virginia and kept asking them, 'where Kentucky, where Kentucky' until they decided I was the lostest fool south of the Ohio. I guess they took me back across the Ohio so I could be the lostest fool north of the Ohio."

"Was it real rough up there?"

"No. Not too much. Every now and then, I'd go up to some of them and ask them 'where Kentucky, where Kentucky' and they would laugh like I'd just said the funniest thing they had ever heard. Once I got on a horse and pointed northeast and said Kentucky. Since no one tried to stop me, I rode around the village three times and then put the horse back where I had taken it from. Someone asked where I had been and I told them Kentucky. After that, they would bring me a horse and tell me 'go Kentucky' and I'd ride the horse around for an hour or so and tell them I had been to Kentucky. Every Shawnee there thought I was either the dumbest or the funniest white man they had ever saw. Maybe I was. Have you got any food?"

Simon Tyrie got some cold meat and cold fried corn bread from his wallet and handed it to me. It wasn't much but I was hungry and after four days of berries, it was probably not much more or less than I should have eaten right then. It might not have been the best food I had ever ate but I was grateful for it right then. After I finished wolfing it down George Tyrie handed me a canteen. The canteen was about two thirds full and I didn't stop drinking until I had finished drinking all the water in the canteen. After eating and drinking I went right back to telling them the story of my time with the Shawnee.

"Like I said, it wasn't a hard life and I wasn't abused none but two things happened. The first thing is that a family had adopted Joe Jackson. I think he was captured while they were making salt at the Blue Licks. Anyway, Joe kept eyeing me and talking to his adopted family. The second reason for risking an escape is that the Shawnee are putting together a force of over five hundred Indians and British to come attack Boonesborough. Heard some talking of bringing a cannon from Detroit"

"Damn!" Simon Tyrie was suddenly paying serious attention. "How soon will they be here?"

"I don't know. How far are we from Boonesborough?"

"Less than half a mile?"

"What? We are less than half a mile from Boonesborough! No wonder I thought things were beginning to feel familiar. I was afraid that traveling at night, I might get lost. We have to get moving now.

I was tired, weak and sore but I had eaten. I was able to

stand up by using my walking stick. I was in a hurry. "Let's go. Why are we waiting? Why are wasting time out here? I left my wife in that fort. Let's go."

"Samuel, why don't we let Simon go on ahead and let everybody know that we are bringing in a white man that looks like an Injun? That way folks won't get scared and nobody will shoot you by mistake."

I had a notion that George had some other reasons to send Simon ahead but I nodded and went along with the idea. I got the notion right then that I should make sure I was awake and a little more alert before we got to the fort. I had had a few hours rest and some food but I knew that I was not fully alert and I knew that I was still tired and weak. The trick might be not letting anyone else guess how bad a shape I was in. It made sense that Simon going on ahead could start warning the fort quicker.

Simon started back to the fort but stopped, turned around and stared at me.

"Damn, Samuel, everybody thinks you are dead. Even your wife thinks that you are dead. Folks are sure going to be some surprised at you coming back from the dead and all."

"They'll get over it."

Walking slow to the fort, slower than I had walked in many years, I wondered what had changed at Boonesborough. New folks like George and Simon would have arrived. The whole salt making party had been captured. One thing was for sure, the world didn't stop just because a man got captured by the Shawnee. I started to ask George what had changed but I had e gotten a gut feeling that there were things that George didn't want to talk to me about. Maybe not about all the changes but some of the changes. There was only one change I was concerned about. I got a sudden fear that Patsy might have died. The thought hit me like a kick in the gut.

"George, I'm getting the notion that you don't want to tell me a lot but I have one question to ask you. You answer this one question and I won't ask you anymore. Is Patsy alive and at Fort Boonesborough?"

"Well that is kind of two questions but yes. Yes. Patsy is alive and yes Patsy is still at Boonesborough.

"Good."

Relieved, I smiled and thought, "Good. As long as Patsy is alive, everything will be okay. It won't matter if half the fort fell down as long as Patsy is alive and well. I had grown aware during my captivity that I had viewed himself as her protector more than her lover. It had hurt me deeply to see her as a bound girl, an indentured servant without the ability to make and carry out most decisions without permission. It had occurred to me two months into my captivity by the Shawnee that in my role as protector, that I had also limited the decisions that she could make.

I knew that during my captivity that I had played a role that eventually allowed me to escape. He wondered if Patsy had played a role during her indenture and if she was playing a role with me. The thought that she would feel it necessary to play such a role galled me but I had seen others play such roles. Beyond the shadow of a doubt, I knew that anything other than playing the role I had played to the Shawnee would likely have resulted in my getting killed. I had seen a belligerent captive killed and could do nothing to stop the killing, nothing that wouldn't have gotten me killed too.

I was tired, sore and hungry, but I had discovered in me a newfound, deep and real appreciation of independence and the need to pick when and where to fight. I had also come to realize that noble actions could be misinterpreted. He had felt good and noble when I had paid off Patsy's indenture. I looked at it as freeing her but, not wanting to appear a braggart, had never told her how good it felt to free her.

Like I said, I still had a gut feeling that George was holding back telling me everything that was going on at Boonesborough. I knew that I had promised to ask only one question but I figured that if I made it a statement that then I wouldn't be going back on my word. I made my question into a statement.

"I reckon that everybody at Boonesborough will be pretty durn glad to see me."

George hesitated a bit before he gave me his answer.

"I reckon, of course there's always a few rotten apples."

"It's best to make cider before the apple gets rotten and to separate the rotten apples before they spoil the good apples."

"I reckon."

I could see that George was a fair man and did not like to take sides. I could also see that he had been some tore up about how much he should tell me. I noticed that it started as soon as he learned who I was. When we got within sight of the fort could tell that he had made up his mind. He stopped, turned to face me and looked me right in the eyes and began to talk.

"Samuel, we got new settlers in Boonesborough. Of course, you know that Simon and me are new. Another new settler came in when we did. His name is Kurt Schmidt. Kurt is a bully. He is mean and he fights to win. What I mean is he don't fight fair. I have seen him challenge a man to a fight and tell the man to take off his coat or to lay something down. When the man turns or moves to take off his coat or to lay something down, Kurt jumps them. Kurt likes to hurt people.

"I don't know much about Kurt. He came to Virginia from Pennsylvania. He never said where in Pennsylvania but someone had heard read in a Philadelphia newspaper that a German by the name of Karl Schneider was wanted by the law for murdering a man with his bare hands and robbing him. There was a description in the newspaper that fit Kurt to a T. Nobody ever accused him of the crimes because he is a dangerous man. He generally just takes what he wants.

Remember, if you don't remember nothing else, that Kurt is a dangerous and tricky man.

This was good information to have. On the Kentucky Frontier, a challenge had to be answered if a man wanted to continue living in the community. A man who was considered a coward could not and would not be depended on in an emergency. Frontier fights sometimes ended with ears bitten off, broken bones and eyes gauged out. Sometimes fights occurred over simple disagreements.

Careful not to ask a question, Samuel remarked, "I reckon you know what this Kurt's weakness is George."

George hesitated before answering. "I am not sure he has a weakness but I think he is afraid of dogs."

I figured that was good information to know too. I knew that if I was attacked that Bull join in without being asked. At least, he had before. Judging from his actions when they found me, he would again.

There was a crowd waiting when we got to the gate. Ben Taylor walked out to meet me. I wondered where Patsy was. Ben grabbed me by the arm and said, "Welcome back."

Others were crowding around me. Colonel Richard Callaway, who fancied himself as something of a big he-coon of the fort came up to me and shook my hand. I saw a lot of people but I didn't see Patsy.

I saw Daniel and Squire Boone standing off to one side a little behind a large man who was standing holding a rifle. As I noticed them, Bull must have saw them too because he began to bristle and growl. I was pretty sure he wasn't growling at the

Boones.

While I watched, the man holding the rifle raised it to his shoulder and pointed it at me. Squire Boone, who I noticed was lamed and using a walking stick, knocked the rifle barrel downward with his walking stick and shouted, "None of that."

The rifle fired into the ground causing everyone to turn to the three men.

"I was just going to kill the dog."

"It aint your dog to kill."

"Mine as much as anybody's."

It was then that I saw Patsy. I almost didn't recognize her. To start with, there was a bruise on her face. She looked scared and helpless. I had never seen her look scared or helpless before. I also saw that she was carrying somebody's child. Forgetting the man who wanted to shoot Bull, I started toward her.

When I started walking toward Patsy, the crowd started moving with me. Ben and two others stayed real close. I tried to hurry but I was weak and still couldn't move real fast. A growling Bull stalked in front of me. Before I reached Patsy, she started walking toward me but she was stopped when the man who had tried to shoot Bull grabbed her and jerked her to him. It was then that I heard George Tyrie speak to me.

"Samuel that is Kurt."

That answered a lot of questions for me. It told me why the Tyrie's hadn't been eager to answer questions and why Patsy now had a bruised face. It told me why George had given me so much information about a man known as Kurt Schmidt.

I knew that I was in no shape for a fight right then but I also knew that I probably couldn't avoid a fight and still live with myself. I figured that catching him off guard might be my best bet.

25

"Karl, turn loose of my wife."

He was caught off guard. I don't know what he was expecting but he hadn't expected to be called Karl. It distracted him to the point that Patsy was able to pull away, ripping her dress as she did.

"What do you mean Karl? MY Name is Kurt. I'm Kurt Schmidt."

"No you aint. You are Karl Schneider. You are a murderer. You're a thief and you're a liar. That all adds up to you are a coward."

"Coward! We'll see who the coward is right now. Just put down your stick and tie up your dog. We'll see who the coward is in this fort. We'll fight right now."

Patsy reached my side. She was crying and sobbing. I could see that she had more and older bruises.

"Don't fight him Samuel, he'll kill you."

I had been in fights. Both wrestling and fights with Chickamauga that had got down to hand to hand, knife and tomahawk affairs where, usually, no more than one walked away. I had wrestled with the Shawnee when I was their captive but with them I always made sure I lost, then I would ask them, "Where Kentucky." I had never been in a fight in the condition I was in right then. Tired and having fled more than a hundred and miles from the Shawnee in four days. Weak from having one meal during that time that wasn't berries.

I took this time to study Kurt or Karl or whoever the hell he was. Tall, big, and brawny; he looked like a man who had been in a lot of fights. He also looked like he wasn't used to losing. Just looking at him, I figured he was the type of man who always had the odds in his favor. He seemed to me to be a man who depended on the other man being afraid of him to give him an advantage. He reminded me of fighters I had seen who worked to get all the advantages they could.

"Bull. Watch Bull."

I turned my back on Karl or Kurt and fully embraced Patsy and the baby she was holding. Then you would have thought a tornado hit a grove of trees. With a roaring scream, Kurt charged when my back was turned. Bull met the charge and got a mouthful of Kurt. I turned in time to see that Kurt had pulled a small axe from his belt and was raising it to swing when two men grabbed him, taking the axe.

The older man, he looked to be in his late thirties told me, "Call off your dog."

"Here Bull."

Bull, still growling, strutted back to my side. Anyone watching could tell that Bull was proud of himself. Hell, I thought pretty good about him too.

The older of the two men then spoke to the crowd. That was the first I knew that he was not a regular at Boonesborough,

"I don't think many of you know us. I'm Jacob and this is my son-ion-law, Hugh. We have nothing against these two men fighting but we would like to know what they are fighting about so we can enjoy it better."

Kurt interrupted, "He's holding my wife."

"Lord how mercy," the one called Hugh answered, "I want to know how your wife got so bruised up."

"I had to show her I was the boss."

"A man has to be somewhere doing something, but if that man and his dog don't kill you, I might."

"I'll fight you anywhere any time and I'll kill you."

"A man has to be somewhere doing something."

Jacob turned to me. "Young feller, why are you holding that woman and her baby?"

That was the first that I had considered the baby might be Patsy's baby. I turned back to Patsy and pulled the shawl back to see the baby's face. I had questions but I was choked up and couldn't get my thinking lined up to say anything. Fortunately, Ben Taylor spoke for me.

"Jacob, you know me. I'm Ben Taylor. This man is Samuel Walter. He was captured by the Shawnee about seven months ago. We all thought he was dead. Too many of us told Patsy she needed to find another husband and too many people told her that Kurt would make a likely husband. He was new to Boonesborough and had a lot of people fooled."

Well, Ben had just answered some of my questions. Patsy clutched my arm. I figured that my greatest fear had been Patsy wouldn't be alive when I returned. She was alive. I figured that put me ahead by a right smart. I hugged her tight and pushed her into Margaret Taylor's arms. I turned to face Kurt.

"Karl Schneider, it looks like you don't know how to treat a woman."

Karl (or Kurt) wrenched free from Jacob and Hugh. He charged me screaming in rage. I moved away from the crowd and braced myself. Just before he ran into me, I pushed my walking stick hard into the ground and dodged to my left, still holding the stick. Kurt-Karl tripped over the stick and went face first into the ground. I landed on his back as he started to get up and got him in a choke hold.

I'll say this for him, he didn't give up. He twisted and turned, trying his best to get at me but I kept my arm around his throat, cutting off his wind until he passed out. I thought about going on ahead and killing him but I got up and walked over to Patsy. I saw that she didn't look scared and whipped anymore. She put the baby in my arms.

"His name is Samuel O'Reilly Walter."

Then Patsy led me to the Taylor cabin.

Bull walked behind us.

3

CAPTURED

I don't know how long I would have slept but Ben woke me in the mid afternoon. It took me a few minutes and a noggin of strong tea to get my thoughts all together. I looked at Ben and waited for him to speak.

"Samuel, Callaway and the others want to know what you know."

It hadn't occurred to me until then that I hadn't told that over five hundred Shawnee and British were going to attack the fort. Well, I had been busy.

"Let's go."

Ben led me to where most of the men in the fort were waiting with Colonel Callaway. I noticed that Kurt – Karl wasn't there. Jacob and Hugh were sitting on the ground. Callaway waited until I got there.

"Samuel, what can you tell us?"

"Shawnee and British, more than five hundred of them, are on their way to attack the fort."

"On their way now?"

"Now or soon will be."

"Are you sure."

"I was sure enough to risk escaping to warn you."

"We've had tales and rumors of attack before now. We aint been attacked yet."

"I hope we won't be but I believe we will be. We will be attacked and real soon. Worse news is that I heard two white men, British I guess. Talking about getting a cannon from Detroit."

The news about the cannon had everybody quiet. They looked at the log walls and then back at me. We all knew that the fort's walls wouldn't stand against a cannon.

Daniel Boone interrupted me, "Samuel, did you see a cannon."

"No. I didn't see a cannon. I just heard the talk. I hope it was just talk."

Callaway jumped back in like he was the one who was supposed to be asking questions.

"Boone escaped with a tale of an attack that got everybody all upset and disturbed. We like to wore ourselves out working on the fort. We aint had no attack yet."

I had noticed that the fort seemed to be in better repair than I remembered. I guess there aint nothing like a Shawnee scare to get a fort fixed. It had needed fixing since before the attack in 1777 but it took a Shawnee scare to get it done.

The blockhouses on the corners had been improved. A

second floor hat jutted a good two feet over the walls of the fort was a good four foot high. They weren't completed. They didn't have roofs but they looked impressive.

"Colonel Callaway, something has been in the making for a while. It wasn't until just before I left that British Officers came to the town where I was at riling things up. They promise to pay for scalps and captives. They have passed out new muskets, new knives and new tomahawks. I fully expect them here in a hurry."

Jacob and Hugh both stood up. Jacob showed himself to be a smart man.

"Colonel Callaway," he said, "I am going to warn Harrods Town. Hugh will go warn Ben Logan. Good luck."

Turning to me, Jacob said, "I reckon you are a very lucky man Samuel Walter. Take care of that wife and son of yours."

With his last statement, Jacob met Hugh who was bringing their horses. They mounted and trotted their horses through the fort gates.

Everyone who had been at Boonesborough the summer before knew why they left. During 1777, what some called the terrible sevens and others called the bloody sevens, a group of over 500 Shawnee besieged the three forts left in Kentucky. Boonesborough, Harrods Town and Logan's Fort had varying numbers of Shawnee around them until Colonel Bowman and one hundred militiamen arrived to give settlers in Kentucky some relief. It was after Bowman arrived that settlers at Harrods Town discovered a camp of over five hundred Shawnee had been camping a quarter mile from their fort. No settler who lived through 1777 in Kentucky would ever forget it.

Callaway was winding himself for a long humdinger of a speech but someone else jumped in before he could get started.

"Daniel, what do you think about all this?"

"Same thing I been saying since I escaped. They plan to attack us."

Callaway jumped in this time before anyone else could say anything.

"Is that the reason you took men from the fort on a useless raid to steal horses?"

Boone looked at him and said in a mild voice, "We need horses."

I could see it rankled Callaway that Boone's opinion was held in a higher regard than his own. Callaway meant to plow a deep and wide furrow in Kentucky and to someday be recognized as one of the prime leaders. I figured that he would get his wish if he lived long enough.[3]

Someone else at the edge of the crowd asked, "What do we do now Daniel?"

Boone answered slowly and thoughtfully, "Most of it, we have already done. The lofts are stocked with corn. We have put away all the food we possibly could. We need to check for more food and store all the food and water we can inside the fort. We need to put out some scouts to try to see them before they see us. We need to check all weapons and repair any that need repairs. We can start molding bullets and put extra weapons where they will be handy."

No sooner had Daniel spoken than Callaway began barking out orders for people to do just what Daniel had suggested. It was certain sure that Callaway aimed for people to know that he was the big he-coon at Boonesborough. I started to get up but Daniel signaled for me to stay put.

"You've not caught up on your rest yet, Samuel. Besides

---

[3] Richard Callaway was killed by Indians on March 8, 1780.

Colonel Callaway hasn't heard the story of your capture and escape yet."

I knew that Daniel put in the last part because Callaway's feathers were getting ruffled about Daniel telling me to rest some more. I could see that Callaway was bad envious of Daniel Boone. Callaway was an early settler of Kentucky. He came into Kentucky with Boone when we blazed the Boone Trace. He was from Virginia, Caroline County or Albemarle County I think. As I understood it, Callaway was never one of the big he-coons in Virginia and would never have been a big he-coon in Virginia. Some thought that he had joined Daniel Boone in 1775 in marking the trace through Cumberland Gap to help found Boonesborough in order to be a bigger man in Kentucky than he was in Virginia. I had heard he was in Kentucky the year before that with ten or twelve men exploring for likely land to claim. This is not to say that he wasn't a big help. He was a big help and he took a big part in organizing Henderson's colony called Transylvania.

In 1776, two of Callaway's daughters, along with Boone's Jemima, were stolen from a boat on the Kentucky River outside Boonesborough by a renegade Chickamauga and some Shawnee.[i] Callaway led one of the rescue parties that went after the girls. I was on the party that Boone led. Callaway's nephew, Flanders Callaway was courting and later married Jemima Boone. Richard Callaway and John Todd were elected to the Virginia legislature to represent Kentucky County, Virginia in 1777. He had been named appointed a justice of the peace and made colonel of the county's militia just the past June. He was rising to a place of prominence in Kentucky but I could tell that Boone's popularity rankled him.

I figured it was my turn to smooth things over a little bit.

"Colonel Callaway, I' be pleased to tell you everything whenever you want to hear about it."

That seemed to make Callaway feel a lot better. He sat down and made himself comfortable and nodded at me.

"Samuel, this would be a good time to hear your story."

"You recollect Colonel, I was to hunt my way up to Blue Licks. I was to kill game on my way up to the lick, dress it and hang it. After I got through delivering supplies to the men making salt, I was to return and pick up the hanging game and bring it back to Boonesborough."

Callaway nodded. He was paying close attention to me so I continued.

"I staked out my horses and went to a spot where I had got deer before. Sure enough, I got a big buck there. I dressed it out and hung it high where it would be safe until I came back for it. A little later, I got another that I dressed out and carried back to where I had staked out my horses. I was going to take this one to the salt makers. When I got close to where I left my horses, I saw sign that someone else had been on the trail. There was a piece of braided buckskin like I had hobbled the horses with. I put the deer down and went up the tallest tree I could find. I could see that a bunch of Shawnee were scattered around the place I had left the horses. The horses were gone."

I saw that I still had Callaway's attention so I took a deep breath and went on with my tale.

"I knew that if they tried just the least bit, they would trail me to where I went up the tree so I quit that tree as quick and as quiet as I could. I figured that the best chance to get away would be to either get to the Blue Licks to warn Boone and the salt makers or to get back to Boonesborough and warn the fort. When I got on the trail, I could hear Shawnee talking. They knew they had me and didn't do anything to hide where they were. There must have been thirty of them.

"I hid my gun, shirt, and gear in a hollow tree. I figured if anyone would come looking for me that they would bring Bull and I knew Bull would be able to find the shirt I had been wearing. I figured that I would be able to run faster without my gun and gear and I figured that if they found me, there was no reason giving them a good shirt and my gear. I figured that when somebody got the shirt, they would get my rifle and my gear too. Main thing was to keep the Shawnee from getting them. A little later the Shawnee saw me. When I saw I was going to get caught, I decided to try something different. I rared back and hollered at them as loud as I could. Then I walked right up to them. I showed them a piece of an old map of Virginia I had and I kept asking them, 'where Kentucky, where Kentucky' until they decided I was the lostest fool south of the Ohio. I guess they took me back across the Ohio so I could be the lostest fool north of the Ohio."

"I reckon they thought I was crazy. Every now and then, I'd go up to some of them and ask them 'where Kentucky, where Kentucky' and they would laugh like I'd just said the funniest thing they had ever heard. Once I got on a horse and pointed northeast and said Kentucky. Since no one tried to stop me, I rode around the village three times and then put the horse back where I had taken it from. Someone asked where I had been and I told them Kentucky. After that, they would bring me a horse and tell me 'go Kentucky' and I'd ride the horse around for an hour or so and tell them I had been to Kentucky. Every Shawnee there thought I was the funniest white man they had ever saw. Maybe I was the funniest white man they ever saw."

"Interesting," said Callaway, "I'd like to know where you came up with that plan."

I had come up with the plan from listening to Boone and other longhunters who had survived meeting Shawnee and Cherokee. I wasn't about to tell Callaway that Boone had any part in the idea, not the way he was rankled by Boone right then.

"Colonel, I'm not real sure where the idea came from, but it was the best I could do at the time."

"What did you hear about Boone?"

"I don't remember hearing anything. I heard the salt makers were captured."

"Did you hear anything about any captured salt makers going over to the Shawnee?"

"Can't be sure. I saw Joe Jackson with the Shawnee family that adopted him but I'd be hard put to say he had turned or was just a putting on like I was."

"You didn't hear anything about Boone joining the Shawnee."

"No."

"Are you sure?"

"Yes."

"Were there any more white prisoners where you were?"

"Yes."

"Besides Joe Jackson, I mean."

"Yes."

"Were they salt makers?"

"No, there was a woman named Clara who was captured around Limestone sometime around the spring of last year and two brothers younger than me."

"Why didn't you try to bring them with you?"

It was time to wander from the truth a little piece. The two brothers had been adopted into a Shawnee family and I wasn't all that sure that they wanted to leave. I would like to have brought Clara back but she wouldn't leave her two month old half

Shawnee baby behind. She wasn't eager to take it to a place where a lot of white people were either.

"There wasn't a chance to get them. Everything happened real quick. I found out about the raid coming up and happened upon a horse and I lit out. There wasn't time to fix up anything real fancy."

"Are you sure that you didn't hear anything about Boone turning Indian."

"I'm sure but if they thought he was turning Injun, then it's because he fooled them like I did."

Callaway took a step toward me with a finger raised. That was as far as he got. A low rumbling growl from Bull stopped him in his tracks. Callaway backed up and Bull stopped growling. I come in a hair of telling Callaway what I thought of him trying to get me to say something against Boone but I figured we would have enough fighting to do soon enough without stirring up trouble between us.

"Colonel Callaway, if it's all the same to you, I am plumb tuckered out and could use some more vittles and rest."

Callaway nodded. I could tell that he liked to be called colonel. With Bull walking guard duty on me, I returned to Ben Taylor's cabin.

4

BOONE'S STORY

Daniel was waiting for me when I woke up. The day was starting to cool down so I reckoned that it was late. I was still a little wore out I guess because I noticed the cool before I noticed that it was getting dark outside. As I woke, I saw that Daniel had Squire with him.

Daniel Boone was the true leader of the fort. The Indian presence during 1777 kept us from getting enough supplies laid back. By Christmas we were almost out of salt. On the first day of the New Year, the 1st day of January, 1778, Boone took a party of thirty settlers to the Blue Licks, on the Licking River, to make salt for the different forts and stations in Kentucky.

It was while taking supplies to these men that I was captured by the Shawnee. I wasn't the only one captured. In early February, while Boone was hunting for meat to feed the salt makers, he stumbled up on a party of over one hundred Shawnee and two Frenchmen marching against the unsuspecting settlers at Fort Boonesborough. The Shawnee saw Boone as soon as he saw them.

The Shawnee chased and captured Boone. I had to wonder who captured who. Boone, knowing escaping alive was impossible, surrendered while greeting different Shawnee in the party. Daniel was very cooperative when dealing with the Shawnee, telling them that Boonesborough had over two hundred defenders but assuring them that the settlers had good feelings toward the British. He pointed out that many of the women and children would have a difficult time making a winter journey from Boonesborough to north of the Ohio River and told the Shawnee that he would surrender the fort when the weather got warmer and made traveling easier. Boone also told the Shawnee that he could persuade the Salt makers surrender peaceably to the Shawnee. He also got the Shawnee to promise they would not torture the salt makers or make them run the gauntlet. The next day, Boone and the Shawnee approached the salt makers. Boone told the twenty-seven salt makers (three were taking salt to Boonesborough) that they were outnumbered and surrounded and that escape was impossible. He persuaded them that surrender was their only real choice. The twenty-seven salt makers wisely surrendered without resistance.

Boone had got the Shawnee to promise good treatment to all the salt makers who would surrender peacefully. The Shawnee kept their promise concerning the good treatment of the twenty-seven salt makers. However, no such promise had been made concerning Boone and Daniel had to run the Gauntlet. Running the gauntlet was running between two rows of Shawnee, each Shawnee holding a stick. Boone turned the ordeal into an advantage by butting his head into a Shawnee's stomach and taking his stick from him. He ran the remainder of the Gauntlet flailing with the stick.

Boone and the other prisoners were taken to Old Chillicothe, the principal Shawnee town on Little Miami River. The trip was uncomfortable in severe winter weather which delayed their trip making it a ten day trip. Although the trip was rough and uncomfortable, the prisoners were not badly treated. Less than three weeks later, Boone and ten of the salt makers were taken by almost fifty Shawnee to Detroit. They arrived around three weeks later. At Detroit, Governor Hamilton, the British commander and scalp buyer, to Boone's surprise, treated him very humanely. Hamilton asked how the fort came to run out of salt and Boone told him the forts in Kentucky had all been reinforced and had ran out of salt as a result. He added that Boonesborough now had two hundred defenders.[4]

During the trip, the Shawnee appeared to enjoy having Boone with them. Boone, wisely, did nothing to anger the Shawnee or to make it appear he did not enjoy being with them. He was very friendly and personable when speaking to Governor Henry Hamilton. Hamilton tried unsuccessfully to buy Boone from the Shawnee but the Shawnee liked Boone too much to let him go.

Boone made friends with several English gentlemen at Detroit. These Englishmen generously offered personal loans to Boone so that he could make his captivity more comfortable. Boone thanked them for their offers but explained that he would not be able to repay their kindnesses. Boone impressed the British who viewed him as both unique and someone who could bring the Kentucky settlements into the British fold.

The Shawnee left the ten salt makers as captives with the British at Detroit and returned with Boone to Old Chillicothe, where they arrived in late April. Although the trip was long and tiring, Boone noted that it was through rich, fertile country that was well watered by many fine springs and streams of water.

After returning to Chillicothe, Boone was careful not to irritate the Shawnee and was accepted by the Shawnee. He was adopted, according to the Shawnee custom, by Blackfish the leader. He became an adopted son and received a great deal of attention from his Shawnee family.

Boone took pains to be friendly with his captors and/or his adoptive family. He was careful to always appear to be very familiar and friendly with them. He was always cheerful and

---

[4] Less than a year later, Hamilton was surrendering the fort at Vincennes to George Rogers Clark.

carefree. This ploy caused the Shawnee to have a great deal of confidence in Boone.

Boone repaired their broken muskets and engaged in shooting matches with the Shawnee. At the shooting matches, He was always careful to make sure that he finished no better than second. He felt that if he won the matches outright he might cause some of the Shawnee to be jealous of his skill. I agreed with him. This fear of causing jealousy was the reason that I took pains never to win a wrestling match with a Shawnee.

Blackfish, the Shawnee leader liked and respected Boone as well as valuing Boone's friendship. He showed Boone so much trust that he furnished him with a firearm and ammunition so he could hunt alone. Boone usually returned with wild game which he always presented to Blackfish. Boone lived as good as the Shawnee lived, eating what they ate and sleeping in the same homes they slept in. Boone wondered sometimes if the Shawnee were fooling him just as he was trying to fool them. After all, they were counting on Daniel to talk the settlers at Boonesborough into surrendering the fort to the Shawnee.

Daniel Boone was no fool and took pains to hide these doubts from the Shawnee. So far as any Shawnee could tell, Boone was very content with his lot with the Shawnee. The truth was, he was looking for a chance to make his escape. He did everything he could to avoid getting the Shawnee suspicious of his motives.

In June, Boone was taken to the salt springs on the Scioto River where he was kept busy making salt for ten days. When he was not making salt, Boone hunted and formed an opinion of the land. He found the land to be rich and rolling. He also noted that it was well watered.

Boone returned to Chillicothe to discover over four hundred and fifty Indians painted and ready to march against Boonesborough. The group contained the tribe's best warriors and they were well armed with British supplied trade guns.

While taking care to display none of his feelings or alarm, Boone determined to escape the first opportunity. His chance came halfway through July. He left before daybreak and traveled, as I had, with a minimum of food and rest for four days on a journey of over one hundred fifty miles to Boonesborough. Like me, Boone was mistaken for an Indian when he arrived at Boonesborough,

He found the fort in need of repair and sounded the alarm that resulted in immediate repairs being done. The gates and posterns were strengthened and made solid. The walls were strengthened and the blockhouses further fortified. This was finished in ten days. During these ten days, the settlers feared the immediate arrival of the Shawnee.

William Hancock, a second prisoner of the Shawnee escaped to the fort. He arrived naked, half-starved and exhausted after three weeks travel. The Shawnee had taken his clothing each night in an effort to discourage escaping. He swam across the Ohio River but was carried so far downstream that he became lost. He reported that the Shawnee were delaying their march because Boone had escaped. The Indians had sent scouts out to check Boonesborough and the strengthening of the fort was viewed with some alarm.

Hancock brought alarming news to Boonesborough. There was talk among the Shawnee of Cannon being brought from Kentucky to attack the settlers. Everyone had confidence in their ability to hold the fort against the Shawnee but had no illusions in the fort's ability to stand against cannons. The worst part about cannon was that there was no time to make the fort strong enough to resist cannon fire.

In early August, Boone led a party of nineteen men to steal horses from a small village on the Scioto River. Four miles from the village, they ran into a larger body of Shawnee on their way to Chillicothe to join the attack on Boonesborough. A fight started which cost the Shawnee a few warriors but Boone decided that taking what was available (three horses, and all their baggage) and returning to Kentucky was the best course of action.

They returned to Boonesborough with haste and had been waiting for an attack until I arrived.

"You caught up on your sleep yet?"

"Don't know. Maybe."

"Probably not. It'll take a while."

"Probably."

"You come back to some changes."

"I sure didn't expect you to come back to find my wife married to someone else."

"It could be worse, I came back to find that Rebecca returned to Virginia or North Carolina."

"I didn't know."

"No way you could have known. She thought I was dead and went back east. Things happen quick out here. They have to happen quick and women don't have it easy, especially when they are carrying a baby."

I couldn't think of anything to say. I felt that I had failed Patsy by putting myself in a situation where I could be captured. I figured that I had done something stupid.

"In a way, you are lucky. She married a man that didn't deserve her and didn't treat her right. Probably because she was so sad thinking she had lost you that she wasn't thinking straight. If she had married a good man, she might have got attached to him."

"Maybe."

I wondered what Patsy must have felt when they told her I was dead. Alone on the Kentucky frontier, it must have been hard to face.

Daniel interrupted my thoughts with another question.

"Samuel, what do you think of that fine baby of yours?"

"Baby? Mine?

"Can't you count? That baby is close to two months old and you were only gone a little over seven months. You need to start making a big fuss over that young'un. Women don't take it kindly when the pappy don't make a big fuss over the baby."

"Thanks Daniel. I guess my brain has been too tired to work right. Where's Patsy now?"

"She's outside with Margaret. She didn't want to take a chance on his crying waking you up."

I got up and adjusted my breechclout. It was the only clothing I had to wear. It hadn't bothered me when I was with the Shawnee but here with white women it made me feel a little naked.

I left the cabin in front of Daniel and walked to where Patsy was holding my son. I didn't know what to do so I sat down beside her and took my son from her arms and held him.

Patsy picked up a large basket. It had bedding in it so I figured it was where the baby slept. She removed a cushion or pillow from the basket and began pulling loose the threads at one end. It took a few minutes but she finished the job and putting her hand inside the cushion, pulled out some of the stuffing. Smiling with tears in her eyes, she shook it out. She handed it to me and I kind of choked up. It was the same Linsey-Woolsey shirt that I had left inside the hollow of the tree with my rifle and gear.

I tried to say something but I was too choked up to talk.

45

I have got to admit that I felt sort of helpless. I was holding the son I had helped to create and just holding him made me feel so indebted to the woman that was sitting beside me that I was afraid to say anything.

I didn't know that I was crying until Patsy wiped tears from my face.

"It's going to be okay, Samuel. Everything is going to be okay."

"I know."

"You're back. I'm yours. We're a family."

"I know."

"I'm sorry I thought you were dead?"

"Everybody thought I was dead."

"I shouldn't have married Kurt."

"Better him than someone who was worth a damn."

"What?"

"If you had married a good man, you might not want me back."

Patsy held and caressed me while I held our baby. I realized that she was crying now, silently at first then sobbing.

There were people around us. They were all going about their business and trying not to intrude on us. Ben and Colonel Callaway and two other men went to a three sided lean-to, stooped and entered it. A few minutes later they approached us. I saw that they carried my rifle and gear. They didn't have any of my clothing, but then again I never had much in the way of clothes.

I put the Linsey-Woolsey shirt on while they were walking up. It fit a little looser than the last time I wore it. It came to the top of my knees and with it on I didn't feel near as naked. If I could come up with a belt, I'd be set.

Colonel Callaway spoke, "We think you should have your belongings returned to you."

"Thanky Colonel."

"We will have to talk again."

"I nodded and wondered what he wanted to talk about.

Exaggerating numbers by having women dress as men. Photo by Jim Cummings of graphicenterprises.net

5

SIEGE

DAY 1

The day after I returned to Boonesborough started like a regular day. Squire Boone's sons were posted on horseback where they had a clear view of anyone who tried to sneak up on the fort. The women were doing the woman work that I don't reckon I'll ever understand. The younger children were being watched by some of the half-growed girls while they were playing outside the fort's gate. The men were all restless because we had little that we could do while we had to stay close to the fort. Some of us were taking turns digging a well inside the fort but we weren't making a lot of progress.

The men were restless because nobody likes make-work and that seemed to be most of what we were doing in the fort. We couldn't work on our farms because two men would have to guard every one that was working. On top of that, we couldn't risk having even six or eight men caught outside the fort. There were less than fifty men, counting half grown boys who could handle a rifle, in the fort and we had over seven hundred feet of wall to defend. We were going to be spread thin enough on the fort walls without losing men to capture outside the fort.

It was late morning when we saw the Shawnee coming.

The alarm was sounded first by Moses Boone and Isaiah Boone, two of Squire's sons. When they first saw the Indians, they mistook them for reinforcements and got real excited. Daniel took one look and told his nephews that the force they saw was Shawnee. He sent Moses and Isaiah to warn the fort. The two boys galloped their horses toward the fort hollering and kicking their horse to greater speed. The girls minding the children had no trouble shooing them back inside the fort gates. The Shawnee gathered just outside of rifle range and spread out. Looking at them, I figured that there was a shade over five hundred Indians and almost twenty white men. [5] I saw that the force was mostly Shawnee but other tribes were in the force outside the fort. I noted that Wyandots, Miamis, Delawares, and Mingos were with the Shawnee. I later heard that some of the white men with them were British but I didn't see any red coats. We figured the whites were French Canadian from Detroit who were hired by Hair Buyer Hamilton.

Regardless of how many, if any, British were with the Shawnee; we didn't see any sign of cannons. We figured we could hold the fort as long as we didn't have to contend with cannon.[6] We had heard the Shawnee expected to get cannon from Detroit. Watching the group, I didn't think it was as big as the crowd hired by the British to pester us the summer of 1777, a year before. Callaway was ready to open fire right then and there, whether the Shawnee were in rifle range or not. Boone counseled patience, arguing that the longer we could delay actual fighting, the better off we would be. Like Boone said, once the shooting starts, our choices get severely limited.

"Well Boone," Callaway demanded, "What do you suggest we do now?"

---

[5] Boone later gave the count as 444 Indians, mostly Shawnee, and twelve white men.

[6] Two years later in 1780, Ruddell's Station and Martin's Station fell to British with Cannon. Ruddell's Station surrendered with the promise of protection. Almost half were massacred by the Indians while unarmed.

Callaway was all heated up but Bone wasn't even sweating. His calm didn't seem to be affected by the big to-do going on around him. I think some of us calmed down just from being near him. Callaway wasn't one of those who calmed down. He was acting like he was getting into one of those got-to-do-something-even-if-it-is-wrong moods.

"Well Boone," Callaway repeated, "What do you suggest we do now?"

"We use common sense. Make the Shawnee think we got more men than we do by having boys and women wear men's hats and clothes. We ignore them and we keep quiet and let them make the first move. We try to delay a fight as long as we can until we get the help that's supposed to come here from Virginia."

We did as Daniel suggested. We dressed some of the women and the bigger half-grown young'uns in men's clothing and had had them show themselves on various roofs and at the firing ports of the blockhouses. We men knew that it did no good to show fear. The women and young'uns, who had more to fear, caught on real quick that showing fear didn't help anybody.

Most of us got pretty restless. Daniel walked among us and tried to keep us calm. He didn't look excited as he reminded us over and over, "Keep calm men, nobody gets shot when the guns aint shooting."

Checking the flint in the cock of a rifle, he reminded the owner, "It's a lot easier to knap flints now than it will be when the shooting starts."

You got to give it to Daniel. He stayed calm. Callaway, on the other hand, was running around like his breeches were afire.

As for me, I pulled me a bench up next to a firing hole and placed my rifle, pouch and powderhorn where they would be handy. After a while Patsy brought the baby over and sat on the bench beside me.

"Don't worry about the Shawnee, Patsy, we'll keep them out of the fort."

Patsy was quiet for a spell, then said, "I aint so worried about the Shawnee, its Kurt I'm worried about."

I reminded myself that it wasn't time to be fighting anyone inside the fort and asked Patsy, "What has Kurt been doing?"

"He keeps trying to get close to me."

"Is it because he loves you."

"I think it's because he wants to have me."

"That better not happen."

"I don't want it to happen."

"Stay close to me."

"I'm afraid of him."

"Patsy, I got the feeling that at the bottom of it all, Karl or Kurt or whatever his name is, is a coward. He would have shot me if they had let him and he only charged at me because anyone could see that I was wore out. If he tries anything, just yell like hell."

The fort followed Boone's advice and waited. We got a little tense but we waited.

The Shawnee must have had the same idea about letting us make the first move. For a good two hours they sat tight and made themselves comfortable. Of course that two hours gave us a chance to see how badly we were outnumbered.[7] After around two hours or so, an African known as Pompey approached the gates with a white flag. Blackfish followed shouting, "Sheltowee, Sheltowee."

Sheltowee was the name the Shawnee gave to Boone while he was their captive. I reckon that Sheltowee meant Big Turtle. I had heard that the Cherokee called him Wide Mouth. The only thing I had heard the Shawnee call me was Where Kentucky. Daniel motioned for the men to station themselves at firing holes at the wall and on top of cabins as he prepared to leave the fort.

"Don't shoot unless they try to take me."

Several nodded but few answered. My mouth and throat suddenly felt dry. Patsy wiped the sweat from my face with her sleeve. While we watched, Boone walked through the gates looking carefree and happy to see the Shawnee leader, Black Fish.

"Cot-ta-wa-ma-go,[8] Sheltowee comes to you."

To watch the two of them, you would think that two brothers were meeting for the first time in ten years. After some talking, they shook hands, embraced and Boone returned to the fort.

"Well Boone," Callaway demanded before Boone was even through the gate, "what was that all about?"

---

[7] The Shawnee and the white men with them apparently thought the fort had two hundred defenders. This was the figure of defenders that Boone gave to Governor Hamilton when he was in Detroit.
[8] Blackfish was called Cot-ta-wa-ma-go or Mkah-day-way-may-qua, by the Shawnee.

"I need a drink of water."

His daughter, Jemima Callaway, gave him a gourd of water. Boone drank most of the water and began to tell what had happened outside the fort.

"Blackfish called me out of the fort for a talk about what I had promised him before. He reminded me with some reproach of my promise to surrender Fort Boonesborough. I told him that I had been with the Shawnee so long that when I returned I was not the leader anymore. Then Blackfish showed me letters from the hair buyer, Governor Hamilton guaranteeing that all of the Boonesborough settlers would be treated real good and taken to Detroit if we surrendered. Then letter went on to say that if we didn't surrender, that there would be no guarantees."

There was a lot of muttering about the hair buyer's guarantee. We didn't have a lot of faith in the British who were offering to buy our scalps. Neither did we have any faith in the Shawnee who were eager to sell our scalps.

Boone finished the water in the gourd and handed it back to Jemima. "Speaking of water, I told Blackfish our women had to get water from outside the fort every morning and that our women are afraid of the Shawnee. He agreed to keep his men back while our women get the water."

"Why that's foolish," interrupted Callaway, "I'm pretty sure we got plenty of water inside the walls."

"There's no reason to let them know everything we know." Boone straightened and continued, "I told Blackfish that I would have to tell the people now in charge about the offer because I couldn't speak for them. I told him that the new leaders would have to talk over the offer and sit in a council about it. I told him again that because I had been gone so long, that I could not make this decision myself. I said we would have to talk tomorrow after the leaders had a chance to talk things over. I reminded him that when I was captured that other officers were put in command."

Boone outlined the situation to all who were listening. He pointed out that there was always the possibility that Hamilton was sincere in making his offer. He also pointed out that there was the possibility that the Shawnee wouldn't give a damn about keeping any of the governor's promises.

"Black fish also told me that they need to kill seven or eight beeves to feed everybody and to tell out women not to be alarmed. I told him that he should go right ahead and that we would probably need to kill three or four ourselves to feed everybody in the fort. He said he would have his braves drive up some good ones for us."

"What makes you think it's just fine for those savages to butcher our beeves and why do we need three or four killed for the fort? It's too warm to butcher meat," demanded Callaway who seemed to be looking for reasons to climb up on his high horse.

Boone closed his statement, "The Shawnee were going to kill the Beeves whether we told them to or not and we need the three or four beeves for the two hundred men the Shawnee think we have in the fort If or when the Shawnee figure out we don't have two hundred men with rifles in the fort, it's no telling what they will do."

"Why," Callaway demanded, "Daniel, Why would they think we have two hundred men inside this fort?"

"Because that's what I told them when they took me up to see Hamilton in Detroit," answered Boone.

Picture by Jim Cummings of graphicenterprises.net

6

TALK

Callaway, Boone and a dozen other men gathered to talk about Boone's meeting with Blackfish. If it had been left up to me, I'd have stayed on the bench by the firing hole next to Patsy with Bull lying down next to our bench. But it wasn't left up to me. Kurt left the group and came over to where we were sitting.

"Callaway wants you."

"Yeah?"

"He wants you in a hurry. You better get over there. I'm to take your spot."

I could see that he was trying to goad me into a fight. He didn't have to work so hard because getting me to fight him wouldn't be any trouble. It's just that right there right then wasn't the right time and place. I picked up my rifle and gear and the basket with little Samuel in it.

"Let's go Patsy."

"Patsy is to stay with me," Kurt interrupted.

"Karl, don't be stupid. If she stayed, I'd have to kill you and I don't have time right now."

We walked away and left Kurt-Karl or whoever the hell he was spluttering. He was muttering something about catching me without Bull along to protect me.

Mindful of the time and place, I ignored him and walked over to join the group with Callaway. Margaret Taylor and two other women walked over and stopped me.

"Samuel, would it be okay for Patsy to come with us? We'll take good care of her and the little Samuel."

I glanced at the bruises still showing on Patsy and answered, "Doesn't look like she's been real good took care of while I was gone."

Margaret and the two women with her turned beet red. First they were red with embarrassment and then redder with anger. Margaret held up a chopping axe.

"Samuel, she'll be okay."

I nodded and hurried over to Callaway's group. Callaway aimed to let everybody know that he was in charge and was talking a good fight.

"We don't need to waste any time talking with these savages. They come close, we start shooting."

There was a muttering of agreement. No man in that crowd wanted to say anything that would put his courage in any doubt. I figured that Daniel Boone would be called on to speak next and was some surprised when Callaway turned to me."

"Samuel, don't you think we have to fight."

I could see that Callaway was trying to hem me in to agreeing with him. I didn't like being hemmed in and decided to take my time answering.

"Colonel, it's funny you should ask me that. You see, not five minutes ago I wanted to fight Kurt or Karl or whoever he is so bad that I almost jumped him right then. I will probably have to fight him. In fact, I hope to fight him real soon. But," I held up my right hand and made sure I had looked every man in the eye before I continued, "I realized that right here and right now aint the place and time to beat hell out of that son of a bitch."

Callaway started to interrupt but I didn't let him. I guess I was still a little mad over having to wait to fight Kurt.

"Colonel, we will probably have to fight that bunch out there. We'll probably have to fight them real soon. But we don't have to start fighting them right this minute."

"Are you afraid?"

"No more afraid than you or any other man here. Hell yes, I'm afraid. I don't want our women to be captured by that bunch out there. I don't want my scalp sold to the hair buyer up in Detroit. We are outnumbered by at least ten to one. Any man here who says he aint got some fear right now is either a liar or a fool."

Callaway drew himself up straight and took a deep breath. Before he could start talking, I jumped right in again.

"You men know the story of how I let myself get captured. They were looking for me and were going to get me. I'd a heap rather got clean away but I could see no way that was going to happen. I remembered what I had been told about the Indians.

I'd been told that had a sense of humor that was completely different from ours. So I acted the fool and gave myself up. I wasn't treated real bad, but I was called 'Where Kentucky' so much that I began to think it was my real name. But I wasn't tortured. I wasn't abused. I wasn't killed."

I stopped to take a big breath and went on talking.

"Whatever we do, we need to think it through and make sure we don't go off halfcocked."

Daniel stepped up and made sure he had everyone's attention. Then he spoke and everyone listened.

"Men, I believe they think we have two hundred men with rifles inside this fort. As long as they think that, I don't think they will try to overrun the fort. If they knew there were less than fifty men inside these walls, they would probably no stop until they took this fort. Yes! We will probably have to fight, but the longer we delay, the quicker they may get tired of all this fun and go back across the Ohio River. I don't see any sin in lying our heads off and making them think we are studying about accepting their offer."

There was a lot of talk but there was no more accusing people of being cowards or afraid. More men were brought to the group and everybody had a chance to speak on what they thought was the best idea of how to manage the problem of when to fight and how to delay having to fight.

I'll tell you the truth, listening to all those men squabble and talk was worse than being a captive of the Shawnee. Some of the men flat out denied having any fear of the Shawnee and others thought that as long as we were going to have to fight and anyway, that we should go ahead and tune up the fiddles and start the dance.

After everything was said and done, we all agreed that we did not trust the British or the Shawnee enough to risk surrendering to them. We all figured we would have to fight but we all agreed that we should keep the negotiations with Blackfish going as long as we possibly could. The people at Boonesborough had sent messengers to both Virginia and North Carolina asking for help. With everybody in agreement, Daniel Boone and Major William Bailey Smith went outside the fort to speak with Blackfish.

With Pompey translating, Boone spoke to Blackfish.

"My father, I have talked long with the new leaders of the settlement. They are very afraid that the long trip to Detroit will be too hard on the women and children. They fear that many will die along the way to Detroit."

Speaking through Pompey, Blackfish answered Boone.

"Sheltowee, my son, did I not say to you that we have brought forty horses for those who cannot walk. Sheltowee, everything has been provided for and your people will be taken care of on the journey."

"Cot-ta-wa-ma-go, my father," Boone answered through Pompey so that Major William Bailey Smith could know what was being said, "I must speak to the settlement leader of this arrangement you have for us. They will need time to talk about it. Let us now smoke and agree to meet tomorrow."

I watched from behind a firing hole as Boone, Blackfish and Major Smith took turns puffing on a large pipe. Boone seemed to be sociable and relaxed. Major Smith looked like he was going to choke on the pipe.

Everyone felt tired and a worn out when Boone and Smith returned to the fort. Several had feared they would not live to return. The relief we felt was so strong that it seemed we could have made bricks from it.

The one thought that most of us had was that we wouldn't have to deal with the Shawnee until the next day. Well, we were bad fooled. After about two hours or so, Pompey was outside the fort again, hollering for Boone.

"Cap'n Boone, Cap'n Boone, Cap'n Blackfish want to talk to Sheltowee."

Boone sighed and ran to the gate.

"Pompey, what does Cap'n Blackfish want?"

"Cap'n Boone, Cap'n Boone, Cap'n Blackfish say his men want to see Sheltowee's women. They want to see Sheltowee's wife and daughter."

"Pompey, tell "Cot-ta-wa-ma-go that my wife went back to North Carolina because she thought I was dead. She is no longer here."

The Shawnee gathered in a circle about fifty yards from the fort and appeared to be talking over the new information. Pompey was summoned to the group and after several minutes ran back to his spot.

"Cap'n Boone, Cap'n Boone, Cap'n Blackfish say his men want to see Sheltowee's daughter."

Flanders Callaway immediately protested. His father, Colonel Callaway appeared immediately to back up his protests.

Boone hollered to Pompey, ""Pompey, tell Cap'n Blackfish that our women are afraid of the Shawnee. They are afraid to show themselves to the Shawnee."

"Cap'n Boone, Cap'n Boone, Cap'n Blackfish say his men just want to see Sheltowee's daughter. She can stay by the gate"

After talking it over, Jemima with Flanders on one side of her and Colonel Callaway on the other side. Boone had the gate opening filled with armed men in case Blackfish's request was designed to get an idea of how many defenders were in the fort. Jemima stepped forward. The Shawnee cheered and hollered at her. Jemima turned a full circle and walked back inside the fort.

Everyone breathed a sigh of relief when the gates were closed and locked without any hostilities taking place. I stepped back to my firing port and watched the Shawnee return to their camp. While watched I felt Patsy come up beside me and place her hand on my shoulder.

"Samuel, everything will be all right."

"Patsy, my darling, don't worry. Everything will be just fine. You don't have to worry."

"That's what I just told you."

Patsy placed the basket with little Samuel on the ground and held me tightly.

Picture by Allene Hayes

7

SIEGE

DAY 2

Thanks to the time Boone had got for us, we began to get ready for both a siege and a battle. As sound as the fort had been made, we worked to make it even better. We placed containers of water where they would be handy if the Shawnee tried to burn us out. We put long poles on roofs so flaming arrows could be knocked loose. Paper cartridges were made for smooth barreled fowlers and muskets. We all realized that we were lucky that Boone and mentioned to the hair buyer, Governor Hamilton that we only had about two hundred men at the fort. The guileless and casual manner in which he delivered this news in an informal setting convinced Hamilton that he had tricked Boone in to revealing important information.

When I wasn't with Patsy, at least three women were. In the close community of the fort, all the women knew that Patsy had received abuse from Kurt. There was a reluctance to get between a husband and wife but that no longer applied. When I was detailed to a blockhouse and Patsy was boiling bandages with three other women, Kurt approached.

Jemima Callaway stepped up to Kurt and told him, "You aint needed here."

"I reckon I can talk to my wife."

"She aint your wife. You got no call to talk to her and you sure got no call to touch her."

"Do you think you can stop me?"

"Do I need to call my pa and my husband and my husband's pa? Do you have any idea how long you'd be breathing if I do, specially after I tell them you touched me?

"I aint touched you."

"Even if you don't, you wouldn't be getting a lick amiss. Now you had better run along while you're still able."

Red faced and shaking with anger, Kurt walked away. None of the women doubted that he would be back.

The women and older children continued to put on men's hats and wamuses. They would then hold a pole or musket and peer over the sides of the blockhouse walls. This was intended to maintain the illusion that the fort was defended by two hundred men. Of course, there weren't two hundred people in the whole fort even if you counted men, women and children. We felt that Boone's slippery comment to the hair buyer was buying us time.

During the year before, which was still referred to as the *Year of the Terrible Sevens* and *The Year of the Bloody Sevens*, we learned that the British were paying the Indians for scalps. I'd be hard put to say who we despised the worst, the British for buying scalps or the Indians for selling them. The knowledge that our lives had a price on them, put there by the British, made us distrust both the British and the Indians. Out mistrust of the red coats and red men was such that some on the frontier would shoot first and never question it the shooting was necessary if they happened upon a redcoat or a redskin.

It was in June of 1777 that we had found Ambrose Gristham shot and killed with the hair buyer's offer pinned to his coat. The offer read "*I assure all such as ...take refuge in...any posts commanded by his Majesty's officers shall be humanely treated, shall be lodged and victualled...shall receive pay equal to their former stations in the rebel service and...shall receive his majesty's bounty of two hundred Acres of Land.*"

An interesting offer but like I said, we trusted neither the British nor the Shawnee.

I don't know where Boone stood on the matter. He was Quaker raised and slow to anger. His oldest son had been tortured to death by Indians yet I had never heard Boone speak of wiping out Indians such as some men did. On some things, Boone kept his thoughts to himself. His feelings about Indians was one of the things Boone kept to himself.

Some men put Indians in the same boat as copperheads. If you saw an Indian or a copperhead, you killed the Indian or copperhead. The thinking being that even if a copperhead wasn't bothering you right then, it could if you got close to it. I viewed Indians more like hornets. I figured that if you didn't throw a rock into a hornet's nest, the hornets wouldn't try to sting you. In short, I wasn't about to look for trouble with Indians and wasn't going to throw rocks at them. If they were after me, I'd try to escape and if there was no other choice, I'd fight them.

There is another thing about hornets. If or when a hornet stings me, I find the hornet's nest and burn it.

Some men who had never seen an Indian close up hated them. In the six months or so I was with the Shawnee, I saw them to be entirely different than I had imagined. I heard them laugh and I saw them when they were grieving. Now, I'm not saying they are just like white people. They are not. Their sense of humor is different. Their idea of land ownership is different.

I was doing a lot of thinking about how Indians think while we waited for Boone and some others to go talk with Blackfish and the Shawnee. No one knew, for sure, how the talks would go or what the Shawnee would do. One of the problems was that none of us, not even Boone, was fluent in Shawnee. We had to depend on Pompey to interpret what the Shawnee said and correctly interpret our answers. There was always the chance that Pompey would make a mistake.

One thing was for sure, Pompey had a bad case of the big head. He rode up to the fort gates on a horse and called "Cap'n Boone, Cap'n Boone."

The fort gates were opened slightly and Boone walked out. "Howdy Pompey, what can I do for you?"

"Cap'n Boone, Cap'n Boone, I got this good horse. A real good horse. I want to trade this horse for a good rifle. "Cap'n Boone, Cap'n Boone, I want to trade this horse for a rifle."

"Well, Pompey, that sure looks like a very good horse. What kind of a rifle did you have in mind?"

A very good rifle "Cap'n Boone, a rifle that got a lot of shiny stuff Cap'n Boone?

"Pompey, I'm going to look at every rifle in the fort and see if we got one that looks like that. You come back here after a spell and we'll talk again."

"Cap'n Boone, Cap'n Boone, I be back here directly. Yassah, I be back here directly."

Pompey rode his horse around the fort and up the bluff near the fort. It was almost an hour before he returned.

"Cap'n Boone, Cap'n Boone, I back."

Boone called down from the wall of the fort, "Pompey, I checked with every man in this fort. No man here has a gun that they want to trade. They say that if you got to Fort Harrod that you will find plenty of men there with guns they want to trade."

"Cap'n Boone, Cap'n Boone, I don't think we going to Fort Harrod sah."

We watched him ride away. There was nothing we could do then but wait. Waiting is sometimes the hardest thing a body can do. There was nothing else we could do so, we waited.

Everyone in the fort was quieter than usual. Everyone seemed to be waiting and thinking. All women found chances to hug their men had children.

Finally, Pompey appeared outside the gates with his white flag.

"Cap'n Boone, Cap'n Boone, Cap'n Blackfish want to talk to Sheltowee."

Boone stepped outside the fort and called to Pompey, "Pompey, tell Cot-ta-wa-ma-go that the people of the fort do not wish to leave Boonesborough and go to Detroit."

There was a conference among the Shawnee and Pompey was called to them. Soon, Pompey came running toward the gate.

"Cap'n Boone, Cap'n Boone, Cap'n Blackfish say good news for Sheltowee."

"What have you got to tell me Pompey?"

"Cap'n Blackfish say British Chief Hamilton leave it to Blackfish what to do if Fort no surrender. Okay to capture fort and ok to make good treaty with Boone. Cap'n Blackfish want to make treaty with Cap'n Boone. Cap'n Blackfish want to make treaty tomorrow. Want to talk with all fort leaders tomorrow."

"Tell Cot-ta-wa-ma-go that we can do that. We will talk tomorrow."

Picture taken by Jim Cummings, graphic enterprises.net

Picture taken by Jim Cummings, graphic enterprises.net

8

SIEGE

DAY 3

Everybody slept light that night. The closest any man came to sleeping inside were those who were in one of the blockhouses. I fixed me a spot at the firing port I had got used to watching. Bull lay down beside me and before it was dark, Patsy joined us. She brought little Samuel out in his basket. She brought a blanket to lie on. I was glad to have her out there with me.

"Will you be able to get enough rest out here?"

"I won't get any rest if I'm inside and you're out here."

"I like having you close too."

"You know, Samuel, when it gets a little darker, we can lie down next to the wall and I bet no one will be able to see us."

"I think you might be right."

Patsy leaned her head on my shoulder and put both arms around me. I moved a little bit so I could put my left arm around her. Soon, she was so relaxed that I thought she was sleeping. I leaned over and kissed her forehead and saw that her eyes were open.

"Samuel, do you think badly of me?""

"Why would I think badly of you?"

"Because I took up with another man when you didn't come back?"

"No, I don't think badly of you."

"I'm glad."

"I just wish I had told you more before I got captured. I wish I'd taken more pains to let you know how much you meant to me and how glad I was to have you with me. I should have told you that I would have paid more for your freedom if I'd had to and that I never considered it buying you. I just thought of it as buying your freedom. I never told you that you are the best thing that ever happened to me and that every day without you is terrible."

I started to tell her more when she stopped me by kissing my lips. I could feel tears on her face as I returned her sobbing kisses. She pulled me over to the edge of the wall.

It must have been over an hour later that I started to doze off. Patsy was already sleeping with Samuel in his basket beside her. I sat on the bench and leaned back against the wall. My rifle and gear were beside me. I leaned over and shook Bull's head.

"Bull, watch!"

Bull moved a little, sniffed the air and lay back down but

this time his head was up.

I was awakened by Bull's growl. From the look of the stars, I figured I had napped for over two hours. I looked around without moving except to pick up my tomahawk. I figured that any Shawnee who put his hand through the porthole would lose it. I noticed though that Bull was directing his growls toward the inside of the fort.

I stood and kept in the shadows, hiding the blade of the tomahawk behind me. I glanced at the nearest blockhouse and everything seemed okay. The gates were still shut. I wasn't sure why Bull was crouching in his attack crouch but I trusted Bull.

Bull was a smart dog. He wasn't so much trying to sound an alarm to me as he was trying to tell me that he was getting ready to tear hell out of someone. Looking in the direction Bull was crouching toward, I thought I saw something in the shadows. It was a movement of a difference in the shade of shadow not ten feet away from me. I was getting ready to shout a challenge when Bull attacked.

Bull moved from crouch to charging with only a little louder growl. I was right behind him as he jumped on the figure of a man. I saw the faint shine as a knife was raised in the darkness and struck at the blade with the poll of my tomahawk. I connected and the knife went flying.

The night quiet was interrupted by cries and curses. I recognized Kurt's voice and switched my tomahawk so that I held the handle near the blade end and swung the wooden handle at the sound of the cursing. I felt the impact of the blow in my hand and both heard and felt the wood strike Kurt's head.

I grabbed Bull and pulled him toward me as several men appeared to see what was going on. Squire Boone and Flanders Callaway reached me first. Ben was close behind.

"Better tell me what's going on here," Squire demanded.

"Bull caught this man sneaking up on me with his knife out."

"Who is it?"

"I'm not sure."

Now I was playing kind of fast and loose with the truth but I didn't want Squire or anybody else to think I was in a feud with Kurt. Still, outright accusing Kurt of trying to sneak up and kill me might be unprovable and might lead some to accuse me of laying an ambush for him.

"Why it's Kurt Schmidt!"

Flanders turned to me and asked, "Did you know it was Kurt?"

I shook my head. "I didn't know who it was."

"We'll get him up to one of the blockhouses," Squire decided. "He'll be okay there."

"Maybe we are all a little too jumpy."

The rest of the night passed quietly. After a couple of hours, Patsy woke and told me to get a little sleep. She promised to wake me early. I went to sleep with my head on her lap. Bull was lying beside her and I got the feeling that he wasn't sleeping sound at all.

Patsy woke me at first light. I woke, looked around me and stretched. All the women were stirring about at cook fires. It took just a glance to see a feast was being prepared, and that a lot of extra food was being cooked.

Soon, the odors of cooking beef was all over the fort. Women were preparing to bake bread and were preparing vegetables for cooking. If the whole situation wasn't so serious, it could have been a picnic. The men set deerskins on the ground where the peace council and feast was to be held. While the men were setting up the council site, women from the fort carried in water from the spring. It is hard to say who was the most nervous, the men on guard or the women carrying the water. Some of the Shawnee yelled at the women getting the water. I guess I sweated a bucket waiting for Patsy to get back through the gates. The other men looked to be as concerned and worried as I was.

By the time the women were through fetching water, every pan, bucket, pail, churn, tub and pot was full of water. Looking back, I don't think any of us were what you would call calm. We might have thought we were but we weren't.

Boone called to Pompey who came running to meet him.

"Cap'n Boone, Cap'n Boone, what you want?"

"Pompey, you need to tell Blackfish that some of his warriors scared the women when they brought in the water and they are scared to go milk the cows. We need the cows driven closer to the fort."

Yassah, Yassah, Cap'n Boone."

Pompey left like he had been shot out of a cannon and within ten minutes the Shawnee were driving cattle up to the fort. Over sixty head of cattle were driven toward the gates. The gates were opened and some boys led by Moses and Isaiah Boone drove them on into the fort.

The boys under the supervision of Squire Boone went to the Council area to finish setting it up. Tables were made by driving forked poles into the ground and placing poles in the forks.

Slabs were placed across the poles to create a crude table. Benches for the key delegates were made in the same manner. Daniel Boone carried out a chair for himself and for Blackfish. The council meeting area was then considered ready for food.

Before the council, there was a big discussion about who would attend the council. The women were pretty strong on the idea that not all the forts leaders would be put at risk by attending the council. There was a meeting and it was decided that Daniel Boone, Richard Callaway, Squire Boone, Edward Bradley, Daniel Wilcocks, Pemberton Rawlings, Ben Taylor, Major Will Smith and John South would attend the peace council. [ii]

Colonel was getting more rankled that people were looking more to Daniel Boone, who was just a captain, for leadership than they were looking to him. Callaway started looking for excuses to give orders. He started by telling the women to be visible above the fort walls after while wearing men's coats and hats. The Shawnee might have thought there were two hundred men in the fort but the truth was, there were no more than between forty and sixty men who could defend the fort counting Africans, most of whom were slaves.

Boone motioned for some of us to gather around him. Between twelve and twenty men sauntered over to Daniel. Daniel looked as calm as though he had nothing more important to do than go a berry picking. Daniel didn't speak to us with a lot of fire. His voice and tone were calm but strong.

"Men, I don't know what will happen. Maybe we will get lucky and make a treaty of peace and the Shawnee will go away. I don't really think it will happen that way but it might. If it don't happen that way, I want all of you to have your locks cocked and ready to shoot."

Nobody said anything but we all nodded.

Boone went to the group that was going to the council and gathered them around him. Careful not to alarm the women and children in the fort, Boon instructed the group, "Don't take any weapons to the council. If you want, you can leave them just inside of the gate where they are handy. Be real careful "

"You be careful too Daniel," Squire told him, "There aint no Simon Butler to pack you back into the fort this time."

Daniel nodded but didn't crack a smile, "I'll keep that in mind."

Moses Boone came running up to Squire as fast as his young legs would carry him.

"Pa, we been a watching from the blockhouse. We seen what looks like guns hid behind some bresh and trees. I swear pa, me'en Isaiah seen it."

Squire patted his shoulder and said, "Good job Moses."

The food for the council was taken to the council place. Those of us still in the fort stood ready to fire if it became necessary. Daniel and his eight other delegates walked to the council area as Blackfish and seventeen Shawnee approached from the other direction. Pompey was with Blackfish to interpret.

The two parties sat and ate. Boone noticed Shawnee hidden close to the council area and pointed out to Blackfish. Blackfish answered that the young men were just curious and wanted to see what happened on such an important occasion. The Shawnee smoked a pipe but did not pass it on to the white men which was not the usual custom for peace talks. This omission caused Boone to be suspicious of the Shawnee's aims. Squire Boone caused some concern among the Shawnee when he mentioned that George Rogers Clark was expected with his army.

After eating the council began. Each side knew that the other had armed men covering the council. Blackfish demanded to know "by what right had the white people taken possession of this country." Boone explained that they had bought Kentucky from the Cherokees at the Treaty of Sycamore Shoals. A Cherokee who was part of the Indian delegation confirmed that this was true. Blackfish accepted this answer and then proposed that if the settlers would pledge their allegiance to the king of England, the Shawnees would accept the Ohio River boundary and both sides would live in peace.

After these discussions were finished, Blackfish excused himself saying that he had to go to a high point and speak to his men. Blackfish went to the high point and presented a lengthy and powerful speech to the Shawnee present. Most of the white delegates knew none of the Shawnee language. Boone knew some words but not enough to follow what Blackfish was saying. Pompey did not offer a translation and shrugged his shoulders when asked.

Blackfish returned and told the delegates that the peace terms had been approved. He then told Boone that since this was an important treaty, a "long handshake would be used." This long handshake meant that the Shawnee would grasp the white delegates above the elbow so that the peace would be long lasting. He also stressed that custom dictated that all present would take part. This meant that two Indians would be "shaking hands" with each white man.

As two Indians began to grasp Colonel Richard Callaway's arms, he saw other Shawnee rising up from where they had been hiding behind stumps, trees and logs. Callaway immediately began to struggle to get away. Whether they grabbed him to capture him or he panicked is not truly known. At any rate, the council degenerated into a struggle with the Boonesborough men fighting to get free and race back toward the fort.

I was ready when the struggle began outside the fort. We in the fort had no idea what was being said but I think we all sensed it wasn't going to end peacefully. None of us in the fort were inclined to trust the Shawnee who were willing to sell our scalps.

When the struggle started, I saw Indians step out of hiding with muskets. I took aim at one Shawnee and fired. The Shawnee fell. I don't know how many inside the fort or outside the fort fired when I did but it sounded like a loud clap of thunder. It was so loud that at first I thought I had badly overcharged my rifle. As soon as I fired, I handed my rifle back to Patsy and took the musket she offered. This time I held my fire and waited until the men running back to the gates were out of my line of fire. I figured to hold fire with the musket until I had a close target to shoot at.

Two Shawnee began to grasp each white man. Photo by Jim Cummings, graphicenterprises.net

I favored using my rifle because I could pretty well call my shots with it, meaning I could generally hit what I aimed at. I was confident that I could hit a man at two hundred yards. The only disadvantage of my rifle was that it took longer to load in order to get accuracy. The ball had to be carefully patched with a greased patch and rammed down the barrel on a charge of gunpowder. The rifling in the barrel was fouled easily by the black powder and made it more difficult to load after a few shots.

The musket was a smooth bore weapon that was not as accurate as the rifle at close range and not accurate at all at long range. The advantage of a musket was that it could be reloaded and fired three to four times a minute and you could shoot anything out that would fit in the barrel.

The loud thunder of gunfire continued as Boone and seven of the men made it back into the fort. One man fell outside the fort and took cover in a low place in the ground. Squire Boone was wounded in the shoulder. Daniel Boone was hit by the handle of a tomahawk that had been thrown at him. Pemberton Rollins left arm was broken above the elbow. The remainder of the delegates were able to reach the fort unharmed except for the man who hid just outside the fort.

Kurt Schmidt showed his true colors as the fight began. He was stationed in the blockhouse nearest the council area and had been talking a pretty good fight, according to the men who were with him. When the shooting started, Kurt was hit by a splinter knocked off the wall by a stray shot.

Just like I suspected and had said, Kurt was a coward.

Kurt hurried down the ladder into the cabin below and crying in fear, got under a bed. One of the girls in the cabin ran out and got her mother. The woman came into the cabin and grabbed a broom. She began poking Kurt until he got from under the bed and ran out of the cabin.

Colonel Callaway had just got his breath from running into the fort and flew into a rage. Grabbing a tomahawk and threatening Kurt with it, Callaway ordered Kurt to join in the fighting. Kurt turned and ran to where the new well was being dug and jumped in the ten foot hole.[9]

No one offered to help him out and the women, knowing that he had abused Patsy, taunted him for being a coward. Some of the women went so far as to dump ashes and rocks on him. Callaway threw a shovel and a bucket to him, telling him that if he was too cowardly to fight that he could work.

Kurt, at first refused to work. Callaway then told him that if he didn't work, that he would be drug out of the hole and thrown out of the fort.

Kurt began digging.

The firing continued throughout the afternoon. After we demonstrated our marksmanship by hitting several Shawnee, they became less eager targets. Thanks to the protection of the fort walls, no one else was hit except Jemima Callaway. A round ball fired by a Shawnee's musket came through a firing port and ricocheted off of an anvil in Squire Boone's forge to hit a kettle and ricochet off again and hit Jemima Callaway on her backside.

Jemima yelled, "I'm shot in the ass."

Flanders went running to her and pulled her skirt up to expose her backsides. A handful of men went running over to see if he needed any help. That was sure a helpful bunch. Flanders was peering at a bruise that was beginning to show and yelled out in relief, "I think it's all right."

---

[9] During the siege of Boonesborough, a Dutchman by the name of Matthias Pock panicked and refused to fight the Shawnee. When the women tried to whip him into helping in the fight, he jumped in the new well and refused to come out until the Shawnee had gone.

Several of the women laughed at his reaction. I took their laughing to mean that they were glad Jemima wasn't bad hurt and humor at his concerns and reactions. Jemima received several ribald comments from the other women. Sometimes I think the women in frontier Kentucky were tougher and rougher than the men.

The fighting continued throughout the day. Shawnees would get outside of rifle range and holler insults at the fort. Dead Shawnees showed that they vastly underestimated the range of our rifles and the marksmanship of our shooters.

As the shadows began to grow that evening, the fort gates were opened slightly and the last delegate was able to enter the fort.

Picture taken by Jim Cummings of graphicenterprises.net.

9

SIEGE
DAY 4

In some ways, we felt better after the fighting started. Without anyone saying anything, Captain Daniel Boone became our leader. It didn't matter that Colonel Callaway and Major Smith both outranked him. The men decided that Boone was the leader and everyone in the fort knew it. I think that it was because we all knew that our best chance at surviving this shindig was to listen to Daniel and to do what he said.

That was another night when nobody got much sleep. A handful of Shawnees came running toward the fort carrying torches but after two were shot, the others got better ideas.

Boone wasn't a forceful leader given to bellowing out stirring speeches like Callaway and he didn't take to strutting around but he did get things done. Walking among us he repeated instructions.

"Be sparing with the gunpowder. Keep the muskets ready in case they rush the fort and have the muskets loaded with both buck and ball. Don't waste ammunition and don't make yourself a target. Try to live through this."

Squire Boone was piddling around with two old rifle barrels

from his forge and gun shop. He supervised as his sons, Moses and Isaiah, made what appeared to be two bellows. Squire was experimenting with the bellows and the rifle barrels but I didn't have time to pay a lot of attention.

After two nights with spotty sleep, most of us were still up and moving because of the excitement of the battle. We stayed pretty close to the spot we had decided needed our defending or where we had been told to stay at. I had gotten pretty comfortable at the firing port near the gate and figured I would stay put until Daniel told me to move.

Patsy had rigged up a lean-to close to me to shade little Samuel and stayed real close when she wasn't needed to help the other women. Patsy had gotten pretty good at cleaning my rifle. I explained to her the best I could how to aim and shoot.

About a hundred and seventy-five yards from the fort were some tall trees that I figured would be turned into firewood soon. Three of those trees had Shawnee in them and they were shooting at the people in the blockhouses and fort just enough to keep people jumpy. Patsy called my attention to the man in the center tree.

"See, there he is, in the fork just below the top."

"Patsy, I think you are right."

"Can we shoot him?"

"If we add another half measure of powder and aim right at the top of his head, we might."

"Let's try it."

I'll be derned if I could believe it. Now I approved of her attitude but I wasn't used to it yet. I watched the movement of the grass and leaves to try to gauge the wind. I looked at Patsy and told her, "Load her up."

"Me?"

"Yes you cleaned the rifle, you might as well do the job."

She looked a little doubtful but Patsy nodded real serious like and said, "I'll do it."

I had to step over to a chimney corner where I had a little space to myself and could water the stones for a minute or two. Sometimes the call of nature can be real unhandy. I had just finished when I heard a loud shot from where I had left Patsy. I hurried the few steps to her to see her beginning to reload the rifle.

There was cheering coming from every blockhouse. Men were shouting taunts at the Shawnee. Someone yelled, "Who fired that shot?"

"Patsy, what happened?"

"I did what you told me. I did the job. I shot the son of a bitch."

I started to tell her that shooting the son of a bitch wasn't what I had meant, that I had just meant for her to load the rifle but I thought better of it.

"Good, Patsy, I knew that you could do it."

"I didn't know that I could but I thought that I could. I aimed just like you told me to aim and I squeezed the trigger just like you told me to and damn, I did it!"

"Oh, I knew you could do it. I wasn't worried a bit."

Callaway came strutting over. "Sam that was a fine shot, a damn fine shot."

"Yes it was. Patsy ..."

He grabbed me by the shoulder and said, "I'm proud of you."

"Colonel ...." I tried to explain that I hadn't made the shot but he was already leaving.

"Patsy, go on and tell him that you did it."

"Samuel, I couldn't do that. Besides, I've got a husband who is a hero now."

Patsy giggled and whispered, "I think I had my eyes closed when I shot anyway."

I told everyone who congratulated me on the shot that it was nothing I had done, that it was all Patsy. This got me a few ribald comments and most of the people thought I was just being s little standoffish and modest about the shot. The more I tried to convince people that Patsy, the first time she had fired a rifle, had killed a Shawnee at one hundred and seventy-five yards; the more people thought that I did it.

Every time I asked and begged Patsy to tell that she made the shot, she would just giggle and roll her eyes.

Patsy had made a good shot but that shot did not end the battle. The Shawnee were not about to quit.

The fort's greatest danger came from Indians who were using the banks of the Kentucky River for cover. The bank or the rivers was no more than fifty-five or sixty yards from the fort. This put the fort and its defenders in musket range of the attackers.

Of course, this put them in range of our rifles too. We were never sure how many we killed but judging by the blood stains we found later, we hit quite a few.

Daniel Boone, despite the wound he had received, went from firing port to firing port and blockhouse to blockhouse. I think the instructions I heard were the instructions heard by every defender in the fort.

"Fire when you see something to fire at. Don't fire just to make noise. Keep a musket loaded with buck and ball for when they try a mass charge at the fort. Rest when you can but make sure somebody is always awake. I think they are trying to feel us out and decide whether or not we really have two hundred men here in the fort. If they decide we don't, there will be hell to pay for sure."

It was brought to Boone's attention that a tall naked Shawnee was hiding behind a sycamore tree. Every time the firing died down he would leap out from behind the tree, dance around and shout insults. He would then turn around and bend over displaying his ass to the fort. Several men had tried to shoot him but he was fast and lucky.

"Well," Boone said, "Let's see what Will Hays can do with ole Beelzebub. Will, Will Hays, come over here."

Boone's son-in-law, Will Hays, came running over.

"Now Will, I want you to get your wind back. You see that big sycamore tree over yonder?"

Will looked through the firing port and nodded.

"Now directly, a naked Shawnee is going to run out and dance around and holler at the women in the fort. Why don't you and ole Beelzebub see what you can do about that?

Making himself comfortable at a firing port, Will Hays waited with his rifle, ole Beelzebub, cocked. After about twenty minutes, the tall naked Shawnee jumped out and began dancing and shouting insults. When he turned around and bent over, Will fired and shot him in the ass. Most of the people in the fort began cheering when the Shawnee went down.

As they had done when Patsy shot the Indian out of the tree, the men began taunting the Shawnee. The Shawnee howled with rage and a fierce onslaught of shooting began. They put a lot of lead into the fort walls but no one was hurt.

Just as Patsy was helping me, other women were helping their husbands. Molly Hancock was helping her husband Billy who was firing from one of the higher firing ports. Molly, like all of us, had missed out on a good deal of sleep. Leaning forward on the steps he was firing from, Molly finally fell asleep. Billy found a target and fired, killing a Shawnee. Still sleeping, Molly said, "Pour it on them Billy, the day is a rolling."

Many other women were equally heroic. Callaway had ordered that the women and children stay at Squire Boone's cabin in the center of the fort. Callaway had ordered but the women didn't pay any attention to his order. Like Patsy, the women helped their men.

Looking back, I think that every woman in the fort was carrying a weapon. Most of them had a knife, an axe or a tomahawk. Molly Hancock carried a six foot long iron pan handle with her. Patsy had a knife and a tomahawk'

Most of the women fired rifles or muskets, especially when there was a charge against the fort. This helped keep up the lie that we had two hundred men inside the fort.

I don't think the fort would have stood without the help of the women in the fort.

The women were loving wives and mothers but they were also toughened by frontier life. Their sense of humor could be and was, ribald and bawdy. When it came to fighting the Shawnee for their own lives and the lives of their men and children, they were both wonderful and terrific.

We weren't fighting just to kill Shawnee. We were fighting for our children.

Picture taken by the author

10

BATTLE

The battle didn't stop just because we made some good shots or because we were brave and deserved to win. The Shawnee knew that the only way they would get a big payoff from the British was to deliver captives and scalps. The Shawnee wanted that big payoff.

The Shawnee kept up a steady attack. Most of their deviltry was shooting at us and hollering insults. We fired when we saw something to shoot at and stayed under cover when we didn't have a target. The devil of it is, after the second day of the battle, I can't say what happened when. I remember most of it, or I think I do. I just can't wrap my mind around whether it happened on the third day or the fifth or when.

Since the battle at Boonesborough, I have talked to other settlers that were there and no two seem to remember it the same.[10] There are probably a lot of reasons for this but I lay it on

---

[10] The Reverend John Dabney Shane interviewed people who had been at Boonesborough during the siege. He found that different people remembered the siege differently. Moses and Isaiah Boone's accounts contradicted each other.

us getting too little rest and that rest being short and spotty. Probably the only people who got good sleep were the children and Kurt. The children got rest because they didn't have to worry about defending the fort. Kurt got rest because he was in the bottom of the new well. Of course Kurt didn't eat unless we pulled up a bucket of dirt and put a piece of cornpone in the bucket when we dropped it back down.

I mentioned that the Shawnee hollered insults at us. Well they did and we more than kept up with them by hollering insults right back.

The insults were about as bad as an insult could get. Frontier folk were not shy and could get downright ribald and bawdy.[11]

Will Hays was particularly good at giving insults. "Yo Shawnee!"

"Yo big mouth white man."

"Shawnee, you know what Shawnee means in English? It means little pecker."

"Damn fool white man die damn quick."

"You sons of bitches better go home before I whip you with switches."

"Maybe white squaws want Shawnee man."

"Shawnee man hell, I thought you was all squaws."

"Maybe white man can't tell squaw from man."

Some of the men could holler insults while shooting, reloading and shooting again. When the men began to get unimaginative, the women would tell them what to say. Some of the women's imaginations would make a hardened sailor blush.

---

[11] The insults were both profane and scatological in nature.

Now don't get me wrong. I remember a lot about the battle but I don't remember just when a particular thing happened or when something occurred. All the days seem to have blended together. I remember what happened, I am just a little fuzzy as to when it happened. A good example is Squire Boone's cannon.[12]

Now I might have mentioned that Squire Boone was always tinkering or piddling with something. Usually it didn't amount to much but sometimes it did. One of the things Squire tried to make was a wooden cannon.

The one in the fort was his second cannon. The first one had cracked after the first shot. Not easily discouraged, Squire started right away building another one. He took a section of a black gum log and bored a hole about two and a half or three inches wide in the center. The log was wrapped with iron bands and chains.

Squire loaded the cannon with a swivel ball and fired it in the general direction of some Shawnee who were out of rifle range. The swivel ball went over two hundred yards and caused some consternation among the Shawnee.

After the Shawnee calmed down and the leader of the white men with them talked to them, the Shawnee began yelling insults and jeers at the fort. Some of the Shawnee even seemed to be making themselves targets in an effort to make us show ourselves. Every time one of us showed them something to shoot at, ten or twelve would take a shot.

Squire noticed that ten or twelve Shawnee were sitting behind a barricade they had made by stacking fence rails. They crouched behind the fence rails shouting insults at the fort while others waited to shoot at anyone who exposed themselves. Squire loaded that wooden cannon with a big charge of gunpowder and around twenty rifle balls. Pushing the cannon log up to a firing port, Squire widened the port enough to put the

---

[12] People interviewed years later gave different days when the cannon was fired.

cannon muzzle through and set off the powder. Three things happened; the cannon cracked, the rifle balls fired out of the cannon spread pretty wide and several Shawnee were hit.

Firing the wooden cannon is something I remember well, but I couldn't say for sure it happened on the third day, the fourth day or the last day of the battle.

What I remember most about the battle is that Patsy took care of me and little Samuel. She encouraged me to sleep and watched when I did. She made sure I had water and food. I remember now, how she fed little Samuel at her breast while I fired buck and ball at a Shawnee charging the fort carrying a torch. I remember thinking that Patsy holding that baby to her breast so he could feed was one of the most beautiful sights that I had ever seen.

Sometimes, when night covered the fort, Patsy would say "watch Bull" and lead me to beneath the little lean-to she had set up. We would hold each other and love like there would be no tomorrow --- which was always a possibility.

Patsy wasn't the only woman in the fort who took advantage of lulls in the battle to love her man. When a couple joined under a canvas or blanket, others ignored the obvious.

At night, the Indians would try to sneak close to the walls and set a torch afire with a flint and steel. They would lite they torch beneath a blanket and as soon as the rosin caught they would rise and try to throw the torch on the roof of a cabin in the fort.

Several times, they were successful in starting a fire. Flaming arrows hit the cabin roofs and stuck. Moses and Isaiah and the other half grown boys used long poles to knock the blazing arrows off but that wasn't enough. While everyone was busy trying to do something, anything to battle the blazes the Shawnee attacked.

The men, me included, went to our firing ports and began firing. Some of the Shawnee were so close that I didn't bother with using my rifle. I grabbed my musket loaded with buck and ball and fired in amongst the charging Shawnee. I turned away from the firing port to reload and Patsy was there to grab the musket and start reloading while I took a quick aim with my rifle and shot a rushing Shawnee. Patsy had finished reloading my musket before I had my rifle reloaded and took a quick aim and fired. She had the musket reloaded for her second shot as I finished reloading my rifle. She fired and I quickly replaced her at the firing port to take a quickly aimed shot.

It was then that I noticed something different. There were more people firing at the Shawnee and people inside the fort were cheering. The Shawnee noticed it too and began to retreat, dragging off their wounded and dead. I reloaded and took an aimed shot at the retreating Shawnee, hitting one as he started to jump over the river bank.

Then I was able to stop and look around. The fires on the roofs were out. Squire Boone had got two of his sons and began squirting water through the used up rifle barrels he had been piddling with. He had a bellows like apparatus attached that caused water to squirt far enough to put out the flames on the roof.

I made up my mind right then that I would not ever again think lightly of Squires tinkering and piddling around. There is no doubt in my Kentucky mind that Squire putting out the fires and freeing people to shoot stopped an assault that would have led to the Shawnee taking the fort.

The Shawnee had lost quit a few in that fight. The high volume of fire from the fort reinforced the notion that we had two hundred men inside the fort. I think that is when the Shawnee began to get discouraged. They might have left then except for the white men with them who were encouraging them to continue. I have heard since that the white men were Canadian militia from Detroit and I have heard that there were some of Butlers Rangers there but I don't know for sure. I guess we could ask the British but they are such liars that we still couldn't be sure.

As I have mentioned before, I have talked with many of the settlers who were at the fort and usually they don't remember things the way I remember them. From their descriptions, a body would think there were forty different attacks being described. I lay a lot of this confusion to the fact that some of the people did not actually witness the event they were describing but heard it from someone else. This is probably very true because most of the time we were at our firing spot concentrating on what was going on outside and didn't have time to go gadding about all over the fort.

An exception to this was Daniel Boone. He passed around all the fighting spots. He gave advice, he listened and he encouraged us. Every time someone called for Daniel with a question, I could see that it rankled Colonel Callaway. Daniel was there though. He checked rifle locks that seemed to be acting contrary and made some repairs. Sometimes he would call Squire over because Squire was something of a gunsmith.

I don't think anyone in the fort minded that Richard Callaway was a colonel, as long as he didn't get in the way. Before there was Indian trouble, Callaway could call himself a colonel or a governor and folks let go as long as he wasn't stepping on their toes.

Now it was different. Most of us figured he should wait for the Shawnee left to start playing colonel. Colonel Callaway was big on giving orders. Daniel Boone seemed to be giving advice rather than orders. Just watching Callaway, I allowed that he would make trouble for Boone if he ever got the chance.

Now we could all take orders. Taking orders wasn't a problem. I think sometimes that we got irritated if the person giving orders seemed to enjoy giving orders too much.

Right then we had a lot to irritate us. Remember that we were sharing a fort with sixty head of cattle that we took in just before the shooting started. We still weren't getting good sleep and could be woke up anytime the Shawnee took a notion to stir things up.

After the assault that occurred while we were trying to put out fires on the roofs of cabins, we all hoped that the Shawnee would seek an easier conquest. Not that we wished ill on Fort Harrod or Logan's Fort, we just wanted some time to get out of the fort and rest.

We didn't get that chance then. For whatever reason, the British and the Shawnee wanted Boonesborough to fall. I talked to Ben about it but Ben was unsure.

"Samuel, I aint sure why Boonesborough is getting all the attention. Last year the Shawnee hit all of us and caused some of the small stations to quit. The whole of Kentucky had three forts; us, Fort Harrod and Logan's Fort."

"I remember."

"They attacked all of us. When they got tired of pestering one of us, they'd go pester one of the others. They were a big irritation but they weren't able to take any of the three forts. Maybe now they want to give us all their attention and get us to give up."

"We can't give up. I don't want to be captured again."

"Well, I aint never been captured and I don't want to be captured the first time. But," he cautioned, "I think we better do our best or we'll all be captured --- at least those left alive."

"You may be right."

I thought it for a moment and asked, "Ben, what's got Callaway running around like he's got burrs in his breeches?"

Ben thought a few minutes before he answered.

"Sam, I think the colonel is a good man. He comes from Albemarle County in Virginia, I think. Where he was, he wasn't on the highest step of the ladder and wasn't likely to get there. As long as he aint put in charge of anything, he's probably all right. He came to Kentucky with a handful of other men to look at the lay of the land and to claim some of it. This was before Henderson bought it from the Cherokee at Sycamore Shoals. I talked to some of those men and they claim he was right handy to have around. He wasn't acting all high muckety-muck like he is here. I got the idea that he is acting like he thinks a man in charge is supposed to act. If that is so, then I guess he just don't know how to act.

"I think Callaway is jealous of Boone."

Ben studied about that a bit before he answered, "You may be right. A man don't know what is on another man's mind but you are probably right."

Our conversation was interrupted by an outbreak of shooting from the Shawnee. We could hear the shots hitting the fort walls but we noticed a difference.

"Ben, does the shooting seem different to you?"

"Yes, somehow it does."

Patsy and Margaret came over to join us. We were used to hearing the gunfire and were somewhat numb to it.

Patsy listened to the spate of gunfire and said, "They aint using as much gunpowder."

Ben and I listened and Ben looked at me. "By God! I think she is right!"

Most of the folks believed that the Creator had a hand in helping us in the fort. We lost two men on the third day of fighting with no more wounded after the treaty council fracas. Each night we got at least a little rain and never so much as to be too inconvenient.

There was a little lull and again we hoped the Shawnee were ready to go back across the Ohio. Instead they hung around. Even Boone seemed puzzled by the Shawnee hanging around. Our questions were soon answered.

One side of the fort was within a hundred yards of the river. The men in the blockhouse closest to the river noticed that the water downstream from a spot closest to the fort was a little muddy or silty. By listening carefully, we could hear activity at the riverbank upstream from the muddy water.

The battle wasn't over yet.

Picture taken from graphicenterprises.net

Pictures by Jim Cummings, graphicenterprises.net

11

THE TUNNEL

We in the fort didn't know what to think about the new plan the Shawnee and the British were beginning. We had been pretty confident that we could hold the fort against a frontal attack. This new attack was a matter of the fort's concern. There was one thing we were sure of, this tunneling idea was from the British. We were sure that no Shawnee would have volunteered to dig a tunnel unless they were promised a pretty big reward for their work.

Colonel Callaway was quick to question Boone, as though the tunnel was his fault.

"Boone, what are we going to do about this? What are the Shawnee up to now?"

Boone was unperturbed by the questions. From the tone of his answer, he could have been talking about the weather. The confidence in his answers calmed the listeners somewhat.

"First off, we are going to make sure that whatever they are planning don't work. Second, let's ask the Shawnee what they are up to out there."

Callaway appeared stunned by the answer.

"Ask them, ask the Shawnee?"

"Sure, Will," Boone turned to his son-in-law, "Will, you been having a right smart of fun blackguarding the Shawnee and getting blackguarded back too. Go up on the wall and ask them."

Will grinned and trotted to a ladder and climbed to the top of the wall.

"Hey'ar you little peckers, what the hell do you think you are doing?"

His answer was silence so began to heat the air up as he started to stir the Shawnee up.

"Hey'ar you little peckers, what the hell do you think you are doing digging in dirt like mole, do you think you are little blind mice? You sons a bitches are wasting your time."

Will continued by turning the air blue with his profanity, questioning the Shawnee's manhood and bravery. This time Will Hays got the answers he sought.

"That you Will? Hey Will son bitch, we blow fort to hell. We blow fort to hell and kill all men. We kill all men and take all women. Women be Shawnee squaws. Soon forget white men and love Shawnee."

Will's answer made his earlier profanity seem like a nursery rhyme. He let go with some of the best cussing I had ever heard. Just when I thought he was finished, he must have got his second wind because he let loose with another batch that was wonderful to listen to, as long as you weren't receiving it.

When Will stopped, the Shawnee started. They told in great detail what they were going to do to all our women when they finished killing all the men. Most of the men in the fort were ready to shoot at them even if there were no Shawnee visible to shoot at.

Boone called over Billy Hancock and talked to him a few minutes. Billy grinned and nodded. He took Will Hayes's place on the wall.

"Hey Shawnee, we know you only say what the British tell you to say. Do the Shawnee need the British to tell you what you speak. Do you know that the women of the British are glad to see the men leave so they can have more fun? The British are almost women. While you are here away from your women, are the British your women?

Soon, hidden by the bank of the river, it seemed that hundreds of Shawnee were shouting insults. While this mutual blackguarding was going on, Boone picked ten of the younger men and older boys and four of the women to keep them busy. Of course, he told the men and boys that the women were there to get them anything they needed.

Boone picked out a stretch of twenty-five feet and had the ten begin digging a trench. The trench was in more than one cabin and to be three feet wide and over six feet deep. His idea was to cause the Shawnee tunnel to end in the trench where the Shawnee could be killed before they could get out of the trench.[iii]

Boone wasn't quite out of ideas. He had the dirt from the trench thrown over the walls of the fort. This caused some consternation among the Shawnee because they did not know what or where we were digging. Boone kept the diggers changed out to share the work.

After I finished my time with a spade, Patsy met me with a gourd of water. I needed the water and was glad to get it. Patsy held little Samuel with her left arm and touched my arm with her right hand. Her touch made me feel a lot better.

"Samuel, are we going to be okay?"

"Yes Patsy. Everything will be okay. It will just last a little while longer."

"I want to sleep all night next to you. It has been a long time."

"It's been too long."

"I don't want to lose you now. I don't want to lose you again."

"You won't."

"Promise me."

"I promise."

I promised but I knew as I made the promise that it would be a hard promise to keep. I figured that we had just been forted up and under attack too long. There was little to no privacy in a fort. If there was a hard rain, there were a lot of people in too few small cabins. When we were out of the cabins, sometimes our only cover was the night and shadows. This didn't stop us from holding and loving each other, it just made for less privacy.

Public or not, I put my arm around Patsy and kissed her. She didn't mind that I was sweaty and dirty. She held me tightly and I hugged her until little Samuel protested.

The blackguarding hurled at us by the Shawnee had a major effect on the women. They shook off any tiredness and began to work like demons. They sharpened the knives, axes and tomahawks they carried. They gathered up full size axes and sharpened them. They suggested keeping axes nest to the trench so the Shawnee could be killed as they crawled out of the tunnel. Those women were as serious and as deadly as smallpox.

Will Hays wasn't the only man who was good at taunting the Shawnee. He might have been the most persistent. Enough of the men in the fort engaged in the taunting to make it sound like more than the handful of men (less than sixty now counting slaves since we lost two men) that we were.

Boone circulated among the men and gave his advice. Boone said, "Don't ever let them know they have made you mad.

Laugh at them all you want but if they know something will anger you, they will gnaw on it like a dog on a bone."

Will Cradlebaugh, hearing Boone's comment about a dog gnawing on a bone, gathered up all the buffalo bones he could find and threw them toward the tunnel entrance. Cradlebaugh taunted the Shawnee, saying since they were working like dogs that they should eat like dogs. He told the Shawnee that they weren't warriors and that all they were good for was digging dirt.

"You are like dogs or squaws, you are not warriors." Cradlebaugh shouted to them.

The Shawnee became angry at his insults and fired at the spot he yelled from until the white men with them hot them calmed down. The Shawnee dared us to try to shoot them instead of throwing bones at them. They said they knew we must be out of ammunition.

"Pay them no mind," Boone advised, "I say we spare the powder until they charge us."

As angry as some of our tired men became, they followed Boone's advice.

Pompey made his appearance again. We figured he was telling some of the Shawnee what to yell at us. Then Pompey would poke his head up above the bank and yell insults. Pompey yelled that any men the Shawnee let live would be his slaves. He yelled for the slaves inside the fort to rise up against the white men and they too could own some white men. Pompey's yelling made people nervous. Several men shot at Pompey and missed.

Will Collins made his way to a firing port. He ran a cleaning tow down his barrel and then another to make sure it was dry. He carefully measured black powder and poured it down the rifle barrel. He put a strip of patching over the muzzle and pushed a lead ball against it until it was started down the muzzle. He carefully cut the patch and used a short ramrod to get the patched ball started down the muzzle. He then used his rifle's ramrod to seat the patched ball on the charge of black powder.

Will shook a little powder from his powderhorn into the pan of his lock. He checked his flint with his thumb and nodded. He pulled the rear trigger to set the front hair-trigger and sighted his rifle where Pompey's head had been popping up.

When Pompey's head popped up several minutes later, Collins barely "tetched" the front trigger and his rifle fired without hesitation.[13] Several inside the fort saw Pompey when the lead ball hit him. Pompey disappeared and was not seen again.

After Pompey was shot, men in the fort had something else to taunt the Shawnee about.

"Hey Shawnee little pecker, where's Pompey?"

"Pompey gone hunting hogs."

"Where's Pompey?"

"Pompey gone hunting hogs."

"Tell Pompey we want to talk to him. Tell Pompey we have a nice rifle to give him."

"You give us rifle. We give to Pompey."

"No. We give rifle to Pompey when he comes to see us."

"We tell Pompey."

"When you tell Pompey?"

"We tell Pompey when Pompey come back. Pompey gone. Pompey hunt hogs."

---

[13] Years later, some people interviewed by John Dabney Shane claimed that Daniel Boone or William Hancock killed Pompey. Neither Boone nor Hancock ever stated that they had fired the shot that killed Pompey.

"You tell Pompey we like Pompey.   Tell Pompey we have a fine rifle to give to Pompey. Tell Pompey we miss him. Tell Pompey to come visit us soon."

"We tell Pompey."

The next morning the taunting began again.

"Hey Shawnee little peckers, where is Pompey this morning."

A Shawnee answered, "Pompey nappo."

Depending on whether the Shawnee were saying Pompey nepaywah or Pompey nepowa; they were either saying Pompey dead or Pompey sleep. We in the fort were completely convinced that Pompey was dead.

The trouble was, we were all dead tired. The women had some of the older boys digging the trench to give the men some much needed rest. The more dirt we threw over the wall, the more concerned the Shawnee became. They would run across the ground to try to find where we might have a tunnel of our own started to attack them.

Meanwhile, we hunkered down behind our walls and waited. We rested when we could and hugged our wives and children while we waited. No person said it that I can remember, but we all knew that any hug, any embrace, any kiss might be the last for some or all of us.

The battle wasn't over.

Picture taken from graphicenterprises.net

12

WAITING AND HUNKERING DOWN

We hunkered down behind our walls and waited. It wasn't that we didn't want to do something to make the almost five hundred Shawnee so away, we just couldn't come up with a way to do it. We dug out trench. We kept people on the walls and at the firing ports. We rested when we could. We promised ourselves, that if we got out of this battle alive, we would appreciate our wives and children and live better lives. We encouraged each other, especially the women and children, and we hunkered down behind our walls and waited.

We knew that at least some of the other forts and stations had been told of our problem because Jacob Hensley and Hugh Mason had taken the news to Fort Harrod and Logan's Fort. We knew that men from the Holston settlements were supposed to be on the way to help us. There were several things that we didn't know.

Simon Butler and Alexander Montgomery were returning from stealing horses from the Shawnee when they had crossed the trail of the Shawnee and British heading toward Boonesborough. Seeing from the sign that the party numbered in the neighborhood of four to six hundred, they made haste to Logan's Fort with their stolen horses.

Butler and Montgomery arrived at Logan's fort to find that Hugh Mason had already reported the probability that a large force of Shawnee were on their way to attack Boonesborough. Several days later Will Patton arrived with news that Boonesborough had been overrun and had fallen.

Patton was thoroughly shaken and delivered a very believable report. He had been hunting away from the fort when the Shawnee arrived. He hid out and waited for a chance to try to get inside the fort. While he was waiting, he witnessed an attack so fierce that he thought the fort was overrun by the Shawnee.[14] There being nothing he could do to help, he made his way to Logan's Fort to report the supposed disaster.

The folks at Logan's Fort, hearing the news from Hugh Mason, Simon Butler and Will Patton all thought that Boonesborough had fallen and that Logan's Fort, with a third the number of men, would be the next to be attacked. Folks at the other forts and stations were afraid that if one fort fell, the Shawnee and British and Shawnee would gain confidence and go after all the other forts and stations.

The fear that Boonesborough had fallen led to Fort Harrod and Logan's Fort to prepare for an attack. It was a wise decision on their part but it prevented any forces from the other forts and stations coming to Boonesborough to determine whether or not Boonesborough had fallen. Neither were they able to gather a force to find and attack the Shawnee.

---

[14] This was possibly the attack that coincided with the fire attack that Squire Boone's water delivering rifle barrels had extinguished.

At Boonesborough, we hunkered down behind our walls and waited. We waited for the Shawnee to attack so we could try to beat them back. We waited for their tunnel to reach the fort so we could beat them back. We waited for help to come so that together we could defeat the Shawnee. It is not that we were impatient but I think we all began thinking that hunkering down and waiting was highly over rated.

It may be hard to understand why the folks inside Fort Boonesborough were so confident that they, that we, would win and survive. We were truly confident that the Creator was on our side. Every night, enough rain fell to keep everything damp. Dampness made it harder for the Shawnee to catch a cabin's roof on fire and easier for us to put the fire out. Although a few of the treaty council group had been wounded, only two men had been killed since the attacks started.

Before the Shawnee arrived, the people had been digging a second well inside the fort. We received so much rain that the only digging on the new well was done by Kurt while he hid at the bottom the new well. It is no wonder that the people at Boonesborough felt that God was on their side.

The bad part of "forting up" was the number of people crammed together with sixty head of cattle. It was a miracle that we didn't allow the crowded conditions to cause friction among us. Instead, we kept fine spirits despite little sleep or even rest. It was indeed a miracle that tempers and nerves didn't start to fray or come apart. There were only a few dog fights inside the fort. Aside from a few lapses, the defenders worked hard to keep their spirits up.

Boone kept encouraging us.

"Just keep it up. The Shawnee aint made for this kind of a fight. Digging in the dirt aint in a Shawnee man's nature. Just keep taunting them for having to dig like groundhogs and it will get to them."

"Hell," Will Hays told his father-in-law, "Shawnee taunting is what I do best."

We taunted the Shawnee and fired when we had a target. We never did figure out how many we shot or killed. We saw some fall but they were not allowed to stay where we could see them. The wounded and slain were quickly dragged out of our sight.

A big worry was that the sounds of the digging in the tunnel were getting louder and closer. Some inside the fort were worried that an assault from the tunnel and at the walls at the same time would be hard if not impossible to stop. When Squire Boone was asked about this danger, he replied, "I guess we will stop them because we will have to stop them."

The tunnel got nearer to the fort wall. Then to top it off, the Shawnee attacked at night with flaming torches. We took up our positions and fired when we had a target. Some torches landed on cabin roofs. It seemed that the Shawnee was throwing all their torches at one target instead of hitting two or more cabin roofs. Women and the older boys watched the trench to be able to spot the tunnel when it broke through into the fort.

Then, to top everything else off, it began to rain. It began to rain hard.

Soon, some of our rifles were reduced to being clubs. In the heavy rain, loading a rifle with dry black powder would be almost impossible. It would be impossible for the Shawnee as well but they outnumbered us by at least eight or ten to one. We loosened our belt knives and belt axes. We made sure our tomahawks were handy and made sure our women had their weapons handy. We told all the women that if the fort looked like it was going to get overrun, they were to go to Squire Boone's cabin and make sure their guns were loaded.

We waited. After waiting for over an hour, we heard yelling beneath the earth where the Shawnee were digging the tunnel.

The heavy rain had not only put out the fire, it had soaked the roofs so deeply lighting them with flaming arrows or torches was made impossible. We taunted the Shawnee and dared them to come. They didn't attack.

Daylight arrived without any attacks. We had all drawn the charges out of our rifles and muskets. We cleaned, dried and greased the weapons. We yelled taunts at the Shawnee to let them know we were ready for them. We saw no Shawnees.

A dozen men rushed out to the garden by the fort and gathered six large tubs of cabbages and rushed back inside the fort. Half the cabbages were cut up and fed to the hungry cattle inside the fort.

There was still no sigh of the Shawnee.

Several men stepped outside the gates with rifles to see what was going on outside the fort.

They saw no Shawnees.

Was the battle over?

Picture by Jim Cunnings, graphicenterprises.net

Picture by Jim Cunnings, graphicenterprises.net

Picture by Jim Cunnings, graphicenterprises.net

13

Battle Won

I didn't really believe the Shawnee had left. I thought it was a trick to lure us out of the fort. I don't think anyone really believed that the attack was over. After all the sleepless days and nights we had endured, none of us could believe that we were suddenly safe.

No, we didn't really believe it but that didn't stop people from going to the gardens around the fort and getting all the fresh garden stuff they could carry. After being forted up everyone was hungry for some fresh food. Fortunately, even in mid-September, there was still food that hadn't been ruined during the attacks. People were digging up potatoes and turnips.

Every man, and some of the women, outside the fort carried a rifle or a musket. Like I said, we really didn't believe the Shawnee had left. Taking Bull and some of the other dogs, ten of us began scouting the area. I didn't so much watch the surroundings as I watched Bull. When it came to finding Shawnee, I trusted Bull more than I trusted myself.

I didn't trust the Shawnee at all. I had lived among them and saw them to be very loving and caring of their families and kinfolk but I had seen them practice cruelty and torture prisoners in ways that I would hate to even describe. The very practice of killing people for their scalps, which were sold to the British, was enough to turn white settlers against them forever.

Some folks have tried to tell me in the years since the attack on Boonesborough, that the Shawnee were only fighting for their homes and to keep from being ran out of Kentucky. No person who was in Kentucky on the frontier would say such a stupid thing.

In 1752, John Finley started trading with some Shawnee north of Boonesborough at a village called Eskippakithiki. By the start of the French and Indian War, the village was abandoned and the Shawnee from Eskippakithiki joined other Shawnee north of the Ohio River. Some folks say the Shawnee were driven from Eskippakithiki by the Iroquois who claimed Kentucky.

The Shawnee were not originally from the area north of the Ohio. According to folks who are supposed to know a right smart about them, the Shawnee started in the south and were ran out by other Indians in something known as the Beaver Wars. The Shawnee were able to set down roots in lands north of the Ohio River in the late 1600's but the only village in Kentucky was Eskippakithiki.

The Iroquois gave up all claims to the Kentucky lands at the Treaty of Fort Stanwyx. The Shawnee gave up their claims in a treaty at the end of Lord Dunmore's War and the Cherokee gave up all claim to Kentucky at the treaty of Sycamore Shoals.

The Shawnee figured that by siding with the bloody British and doing their dirty work for them, that they would wind up with Kentucky. To get Kentucky, not only were they willing to forget earlier treaties, they were willing to murder men, women and helpless children. They murdered babies by taking them by the heels and slamming the infant hard against a tree, and forced the baby's captive mother to watch.

It is no wonder that some settlers in Kentucky hated the Shawnee and all other Indians. Six years after the battle at Boonesborough, I met a young man named Aaron Burns who hated the Indians and British so bitterly that he would shoot them on sight. I heard that he heard a boyhood friend being tortured to death after the Battle of Blue Licks and had no use for Indians since. Thinking on it, Aaron had an uncle or a friend by the name of Lige Black who felt the same since the woman he loved and her whole family of peaceful Quakers were murdered by Cherokee. Lige was a former Quaker who, it was said, didn't miss a chance to kill an Indian. I aint saying I am in full agreement with such attitudes and actions but I can damn sure understand them.

By hiring Indians as mercenaries, the British made peace between Americans and Indians damn near impossible. No settler who buried the mutilated remains of someone who had been tortured and scalped by British paid Indians thought kindly toward either the British or the Indians.

Like I said, I aint saying I am in full agreement with such attitudes and actions. But if Patsy or little Samuel had fallen victim to their savagery, I would have tried to kill them all.

We searched outside the fort and did not find a single Shawnee. Oh, for the next few days, folks reported Indian sightings but I think it was mostly imagined sightings. I think all the Shawnee were gone the morning after their tunnel collapsed.

We looked for dead Shawnee too but we didn't find any. We found a lot of spots where there were blood stains that hadn't been washed away by the rains but no dead bodies. That being the case, we had no idea how many Shawnee had been killed. Daniel Boone put the number of Indians killed at thirty-seven but I aint sure how he came to decide on that number. Even if Boone's count of killed was right, we had no real idea of how many Shawnee were wounded.

Fortunately, only two in the fort had been killed. It could have been a lot worse. I personally think that Boone's having casually mentioned to Hair Buyer Hamilton that there were two hundred men at Fort Boonesborough made the Shawnee over cautious. If that is the case, then I am sure glad that Daniel told that whopper because the Shawnee could have taken the fort if they had known that they would only have light casualties.

The Shawnee's tunnel was a sobering sight. It was a good four feet high and almost as wide. The tunnel came to within twenty-five feet of the fort.[15] An attack through a completed tunnel at the same time attacks were being made on the fort walls would have been hard if not impossible to beat back.

But we won. With two killed and a handful wounded, we won. Patsy came to me and sat little Samuel's basket down. She put both her arms around me and pressed her face into my shirt covered chest.

"Samuel, are the Indians gone?"

"Yes."

"Are we going to be okay?"

"Yes."

"Do you really love me?"

"Yes, I really love you."

I held her while all around us the fort was getting used to the idea that the danger, for the moment, had passed. Almost everyone was outside the gates or near the gates. Watchers in the blockhouse towers kept a sharp watch but I think we all knew the Shawnee, for the time being, were gone.

Colonel Richard Callaway was strutting around and giving orders again. From the way he glared at Daniel Boone, I figured

---

[15]

The description of the tunnel and its nearness to the fort varied depending on who was being interviewed. Like the trench inside the fort, it was remembered differently by different people who were interviewed by Reverend John Dabney Shane.

he was up to some meanness toward Daniel.

"Samuel, are you sure we're safe, that all the Shawnee are gone?"

I kissed Patsy on the forehead and answered her. "Patsy, right this second, I'm convinced that the Shawnee have gone and it's safe."

Patsy looked at me puzzled and asked, "Why are you convinced right now that the Shawnee have gone and it's safe?"

"Because the coward, Kurt Schmidt, is crawling out of the well."

Patsy grabbed a stick and ran to the well where Kurt was pulling himself out. She braced herself and swung the stick hitting Kurt on the head. After Kurt had fallen back to the bottom of the well, Patsy kicked dirt on him.

While women who witnessed the act cheered, Patsy continued kicking dirt into the well.

"Damn you cowardly son of a bitch, I don't want to see you out of that hole yet."

Holding little Samuel's basket in one hand, I hugged Patsy to me.

"Patsy we're safe. The Shawnee have gone. The wind still blows. The sun still shines. The fort still stands and I still love you."

The battle was over.

Picture by Jim Cunnings, graphicenterprises.net

EPOLOGUE

To most of us at Boonesborough, Daniel Boone was our leader and a true hero. To Colonel Richard Callaway he was a traitor. Callaway began court martial actions against Boone charging him with treason. Most of us disagreed with the charges but a few said that some of Boone's wife's people had Tory leanings. I thought this was foolish because the British weren't asking us if we were Tory or Patriot when they sent the Indians down at us. Besides, the Shawnee knew a Tory's scalp brought as much as a Patriot's scalp. I always figured that Callaway was jealous of Boone and that was why he charged Boone with treason and placed under arrest.

Boone's court martial was held at Logan's Fort because Callaway rightly felt he couldn't get Boone convicted at Fort Boonesborough. The presiding judge was Daniel Trabue. Trabue heard four charges that were brought against Boone:

1. In order to save himself, after his capture in February, 1778, Boone surrendered the salt making party and that the Shawnee did not know of these men. Callaway was accusing Boone of betraying the men in the salt making party simply to save his own life.
2. As a prisoner, Boone consorted with the enemy, and at Detroit made a bargain with Hair Buyer Hamilton, the British Commander, to surrender Boonesborough and everyone at the fort.

3. After Boone returned to the fort, he had treacherously weakened the fort by persuading a large party of men to leave the fort on a foolish and treacherously conceived raid to steal back horses from the Shawnee.
4. Boone had exposed Boonesborough's leaders to a Shawnee ambush by agreeing to take all the fort's officers to the Shawnee camp for a peace council out of sight of the fort.

I figured that anyone with common sense would know the charges were foolish but they were serious charges. If he was found guilty, Boone could be hung.

Boone was prosecuted by Col. John Bowman. The chief witnesses against Boone were Colonel Richard Callaway from Boonesborough and Col. Benjamin Logan, the leader and founder at Logan's Fort.

Boone refused to be helped by a lawyer. He said he could speak for himself and that the truth would free him. He did agree to let Colonel Richard Henderson's son, Samuel Henderson and James Harrod advise and help him.

Boone did not dispute any of the facts, which surprised many at the court martial. He did disagree the way the facts were being told to the court martial.

Colonel Callaway used the evidence to try to prove that Boone was guilty of treachery against both his men and Fort Boonesborough by saying that Boone was a Tory who favored the British and should have his commission taken away.

Boone's answer to this was very simple and easy to understand. When he was captured and learned that Boonesborough was going to be attacked, he knew the fort was in bad shape and unprepared. The Shawnee could take it easily.

Boone admitted that he told the Shawnee tales to fool them.

Colonel Richard Callaway testified against Daniel. The escaped captives Andrew Johnson, William Hancock and I testified.

Boone testified to the court that he figured the salt makers and Fort Boonesborough could not survive an attack by Blackfish and his Shawnee. The people weren't ready and the fort wasn't ready. He lied to Blackfish about the strength of the fort and the number of men at the fort. He told Blackfish if the waited, the fort would be easier to capture because it would be weaker. Boone agreed to surrender the salt making party to Blackfish if Blackfish agreed that the men would not be abused or made to run the gauntlet.

Boone explained his friendly actions with the British as trying to buy more time for Fort Boonesborough. He figured that the longer he could delay any attacks on the fort, the better off the fort and the people there would be.

Boone's explanations showed a strong loyalty to Fort Boonesborough. He made a convincing argument that he was telling the Shawnee and British tales and that his actions were the only way to save the lives of the men in the salt making party and Fort Boonesborough.

I was real pleased and relieved when the officers deciding the court martial ruled that Daniel Boone was not guilty.

Boone was also promoted to the rank of major immediately after the court martial.

I could tell that all the foolishness of the court martial hit Boone a lot harder than most people realized. I never heard that he spoke of it again but he left Kentucky for North Carolina to fetch his family back to Kentucky. When he returned to Kentucky, Boone began looking for a different location where he could build a new station. His Quaker upbringing had given him a yearning for a quiet and peace-loving life. Life in Boonesborough where he had been accused of treason soon became unbearable to Boone. Added to his shame, some of the pioneers who had been his close friends blamed him for the capture of the friends and family members who were among the salt-makers at Blue Licks.

Although Boone was declared innocent of all charges and acquitted at Logan's Fort, he became unhappy with life at Fort Boonesborough. Acting upon these feelings, Boone moved northwest of Boonesborough to a less crowded area.

He settled on a spot between Boonesborough and Lexington. Surrounded by rich rolling land, the site appealed to *Boone* as a logical location to settle. With the help of me, me sons and sons-in law and Squire Boone, Boone cleared land and build a cabin surrounded by a wall of poles. This stockade was small enough to be defended by the people living at or near the station.

He moved his family to this station, intending to stay there. Daniel became a leading figure in the area. He became a sheriff, a colonel of militia, and a deputy surveyor.

Colonel Callaway was upset a right smart about the innocent verdict Boone received at his court martial. I don't know whether he really believed Daniel Boone was a traitor or he was just jealous of the way most people favored Daniel Boone over Richard Callaway.

Richard Callaway died angry at Boone. While building the first ferry in Kentucky, he was attacked killed, mutilated and scalped by Indians in 1780.

1780 Was not a good year for the settlements in Kentucky. In June 1780 British Captain Henry Byrd gathered a force of over 1,200 Delaware, Huron, Wyandot, Ottawa, Mingo, Miami, British regular soldiers, and Canadian militia for a large raid against American settlements in Kentucky. They were later joined by Shawnee and the Girty brothers; Simon, James, and George. Captain Byrd attacked Ruddell's Station. Byrd had brought cannon with him into Kentucky and began using the cannon to force John Ruddell, the settlement founder, to surrender.

Byrd promised Ruddell that the settlers would not be harmed. He was wrong. He could not stop the Indians. When the gates were opened, the Indians began murdering the inhabitants. Two hundred men, women, and children were murdered. Byrd was not able to protect all the settlers but he was able to save some pf them. He was able to control his Indians when Martin's Station was forced to surrender and to prevent the same murderous actions when 100 settlers surrendered at Martin's Station a few days later. Burdened with captives and hearing that George Rogers Clark was gathering an army, Byrd ended his campaign and returned across the Ohio River.

Those of us who had been at Boonesborough in 1778 knew that if cannon had been used against the fort, we would likely have had to surrender.

In 1782, a force of British and Indians, again with the Girty's, attacked Bryan's Station. They were followed by a force of Kentucky militia which they ambushed and defeated at the Battle of Blue Licks on August 19. This was the worst defeat suffered by the Kentucky Militia.

Boone led a force from Boone's station to relieve Bryan's Station. We were ambushed at Blue Licks by British and Indians. Those of us who were able to escape the ambush at the Blue Licks knew that we were lucky then too. Israel Boone, Daniel's son was killed there. I remember hugging Patsy real close when I returned to Boone's Station from the Battle of Blue Licks.

George Rogers Clark retaliated by attacking Indians in their villages north of the Ohio River. He gathered over a thousand militia at the mouth of the Licking River. I was there with the militia. Clark led us against the Indians at Piqua Town north of the Ohio River. We attacked and killed close to one hundred Indians. Clark lost 27 killed or wounded. We destroyed the town. We destroyed or took all crops and stores. It felt good to hit back at the Ohio Indians instead of just waiting for them to hit us.

Patsy and little Samuel and me, well we had left Boonesborough and followed Daniel up to his new settlement at Boone's Station. We got a good claim on a farm and settled down for as peaceful a life as the Indians and circumstances would allow us. We now have four children and a good farm.

We were ambushed at Blue Licks by British and Indians. Photo by Jim Cummings of graphicenterprises.net.

An Early Settler in the 1780's

Women on the Kentucky Frontier were strong and determined. They had to be.

Author's Note: Richard Callaway

While new books about Daniel Boone appear regularly, not much is known about Richard Callaway. His apparent enmity toward Boone is hard to understand given that Boone rescued his two daughters who had been kidnapped with Jemima Boone. Added to the confusion is the fact that his nephew, Flanders Callaway married Jemima Boone.

It is said that Lyman Draper intended to write Callaway's biography but he never did.

As the youngest of six brothers, primogeniture would have denied Richard Callaway any inheritance of substance. While he may have had some assistance, the lion's share of effort toward his successes must have come from his own strength and efforts. It is reported that he spent a year in Kentucky before its purchase by the Transylvania Land Company with a small group of companions. During that time, he explored and surveyed land in Kentucky.

Richard Callaway appears to have been a step below the aristocracy of Virginia. There is no record of any schooling he received but he may have had a tutor or home instructor.

There is evidence that he was a capable pioneer. This would mean he was not adverse to enduring hardships or to hard work. On the other hand, he brought a female slave with him when he was a part of Boone's party that blazed the Boone Trace and began Boonesborough.

Prior to entering Kentucky, Callaway had acquired over 6,000 acres of land and he began to be noted for public service by holding different political offices.

During the French and Indian War, Callaway and others heard of the land west of the mountains. Callaway, like others, began to think that his destiny lay west of the mountains instead of in Virginia. He began learning and planning ways to make this success happen. His holdings were such that he was not able to move immediately or even for several years.

In the spring of 1775, Richard was at the gathering of the treaty of Sycamore Shoals. Callaway hauled supplies for the Transylvania Company and volunteered to be an axe man under the command of Daniel Boone.

Callaway must have been considered an asset to be allowed to accompany Boone's party. One must wonder, however, how Richard Callaway felt under Boone's command. Callaway traveled on a good horse and well equipped. As noted, he was accompanied by a female African servant. To all outward appearances, at least, Callaway was happy to serve as one of Boone's axe men.

Apparently, his contribution was significant because he was the members of the Trace blazing party except Boone to receive a grant of land from the Transylvania Company.

Richard departed for Virginia and returned with forty or fifty settlers, including his wife and daughters; his nephew, Flanders Callaway, and other Callaway relatives. His and Boone's examples contributed to the successful beginning of Boonesborough.

After Kentucky was recognized by the government of Virginia as Kentucky County and a part of Virginia, Callaway was elected as one of the two representatives from the new county.

After Boone and the party of salt makers were captured in February, 1778, Callaway became the primary leader at Fort Boonesborough. His actions and leadership had to have an effect on the willingness of pioneers who stayed at Boonesborough rather than leaving for Virginia or North Carolina.

During the siege at the siege of Boonesborough in September, 1778, Colonel Richard Callaway was technically in command but when Boone returned, most in the fort paid more attention to his counsel than to Callaway's orders.

When the Shawnee arrived, there was disagreement as to what actions to take. Some witnesses interviewed by John Dabney Shane placed Richard Callaway at the council meeting with the Shawnee. Some of these witnesses credit him with recognizing that the Shawnee were attempting to capture the men from the fort.

It is possible that Callaway's exhaustion and the stress of the siege led to his decision to bring charges against Daniel Boone. His accusations may have also been prompted by jealousy of Boone's popularity and the preference of the people for Boone's leadership.

Callaway certainly seemed to believe the charges and never forgave Boone for surrendering the salt makers at Blue Licks. Neither did he forgive Boone for leading a horse stealing raid against the Shawnee north of the Ohio River. Added to these supposed sins was Boone's willingness to risk the leaders of the fort in a council with the Shawnee.

Although Boone was both acquitted and promoted, there is evidence that Callaway disagreed with the outcome. Despite the fact he was Daniel's son-in-law's uncle, his friendship with Boone was over.

In 1779, Callaway received permission to build and operate a ferry close to Fort Boonesborough. In March 1780, Callaway with another settler and a group of slaves were building the ferry when they were ambushed by a group of Shawnee. Both white men were killed, mutilated and scalped. At least one slave escaped and brought other settlers to the ambush site.

The settlers found the mutilated bodies and buried both white men in a single grave. The Shawnee escaped.

End Notes

---

[i] In July 1776, a raiding party of two Cherokee and three Shawnee Indians led by a Cherokee known as Hanging Maw captured Jemima, daughter of Daniel Boone, Elizabeth and Frances Callaway, the daughters of Colonel Richard Callaway as they were floating in a canoe on the Kentucky River. An alarm was raised and Boone organized a rescue party. The captors hurried the girls north toward the Shawnee towns across the Ohio River. The girls tried to mark their trail until threatened by the Indians.

Daniel Boone anticipated the Indians' destination and led his party across country to intercept the kidnappers. On the third morning, as the kidnappers were building a breakfast fire, the rescue party came upon the kidnappers. As the first Indian was shot, Jemima said, "That's Pa's gun!" Two of the wounded Indians later died. The Indians retreated, leaving the girls to be taken home by the rescue party.

Jemima married Flanders Callaway, a member of the rescuing party. Elizabeth Callaway married Samuel Henderson, and Frances married John Holder. The kidnapping put the settlers in the Kentucky forts and stations on guard and kept them close to the fort. Although the people at Boonesborough feared the girls would be raped or otherwise abused, the girls stated that this had not been the case and that "The Indians were kind to us, as much so as they well could have been, or their circumstances permitted."

[ii] Different people interviewed by John Dabney Shane came up with different slates of delegates that attended the council's with the Shawnee. Some accounts state that Flanders Callaway instead of Richard Callaway attended the council.

[iii] Different people interviewed by John Dabney Shane gave different descriptions of the trench dug inside the fort.

ABOUT THE AUTHOR

The author, Charles E. Hayes, MSgt, USAF (Ret.) spent 24 years in the United States Air Force. He is a former school teacher and an avid re-enactor. He currently helps other veterans through the auspices of the Disabled American Veterans in Kentucky.

35943276R00087

Made in the USA
Middletown, DE
20 October 2016